FEAR THE MIRROR

# Fear

*the*

# Mirror

STORIES

## Cora Siré

**ESPLANADE BOOKS**

**THE FICTION IMPRINT AT VÉHICULE PRESS**

ESPLANADE BOOKS IS THE FICTION IMPRINT AT VÉHICULE PRESS

Published with the generous assistance of the Canada Council for the
Arts, the Canada Book Fund of the Department of Canadian Heritage,
and the Société de développement des entreprises culturelles
du Québec (SODEC).

Canadä  *SODEC* Québec

Canada Council   Conseil des arts
for the Arts        du Canada

Esplanade Books editor: Dimitri Nasrallah
Cover design: David Drummond
Photo of author: Susan Moss
Typeset in Minion and Gill Sans MT
Printed by Livres Rapido Books

LIBRARY AND ARCHIVES CANADA CATALOGUING IN PUBLICATION

Title: Fear the mirror : stories / Cora Siré.
Names: Siré, Cora, author.
Identifiers: Canadiana (print) 2021023931X | Canadiana (ebook)
20210239328 | ISBN 9781550655773
(softcover) | ISBN 9781550655858 (HTML)
Subjects: LCGFT: Short stories.
Classification: LCC PS8637.I726 F43 2021 | DDC C813/.6—dc23

This is partially a work of fiction. Names, characters, places and
incidents are either the products of the author's imagination or are
used fictitiously.

Published by Véhicule Press, Montréal, Québec, Canada

Distribution by LitDistCo
www.litdistco.ca
Printed in Canada on FSC certified paper.

Poets, like detectives, know the truth is laborious: it doesn't occur by accident, rather it is chiseled and worked into being, the product of time and distance and graft.

–Colum McCann, *Thirteen Ways of Looking.*

An author's speaking of herself is no recent invention. She's speaking of her life, but most of the time she's shaping what she lived through, she's jogging her weak memory, making fiction.

–Kirmen Uribe, *The Alphabet of the Bilboa Museum.*

# CONTENTS

# FEAR THE MIRROR

I AM DEEP into secrets, spying, and magic tricks. I don't yet know that magicians are really illusionists. Hiding in my room, propped on my elbows, belly down on the bed, legs dangling in midair. I'm seven years old and, flipping through a stack of comic books, I study the back pages, scheming on how to send away for stuff, more interested in the ads than the exploits of Casper the Friendly Ghost or Richie Rich. x-ray glasses. Sea monkeys (instant pets!) and a secret spy scope. Hidden buzzers to shock your hand shakers. The invisible ink and pen kit. I dream of writing down secrets and then reading them back in mirrors.

I have no money to buy a kit, but I learn how to make invisible ink and find myself a calligraphy pen of some sort. As an extra precaution, I practise mirror writing, just in case someone does stumble upon my highly private words. Then, when all the adults in the house are downstairs, I sneak into the bathroom with a candle, matches, and my secret words. Stand in the dark, get a flame going on the candle, backlight the paper, and read the writing in the mirror. *Rob and Sandy are bad.* Sometimes I dare to dash into my parents' bedroom with its mirrored wall. This is trespassing of the highest order. *I'm going to run away with Donnie and open a pancake house.* I never regard myself in these moments before a mirror. I don't care how I look. It's my secret writing I want to see. The thrilling reflection of my hidden self.

Hand mirrors or their shards are prized possessions in the sixties. I can't get away with storing pieces of broken glass in the pockets of my shorts like the neighbourhood brothers, Rob and Sandy, do. In the ditch behind Donnie's house, which is across the street from mine in the Montréal suburb of Valois, we assemble a pile of dry leaves and dead grass. The four of us sit cross-legged in a circle and take turns pointing the mirror at the sun, angling for a reflection that could ignite a fire. First time, it's just a lot of smoke. Next time, I bring some paper, ripped-up sheets of my invisible-ink writing, which lights up with satisfying little flames.

"If we get caught," Donnie says, "there's water in the ditch."

We're alarmed that the two brothers are getting carried away. Building fires behind your house is forbidden, right up there with caps and fireworks. Donnie's dad is a bully, a stout man with glasses and a mean streak involving his belt. I'm in on the secret: Donnie, as well as Rob and Sandy, they're all adopted. I'm not. At least I don't think so until my big brother asks, "Haven't you ever wondered why there aren't any photos of Mama pregnant with you?"

I've undoubtedly annoyed him again, taking stuff from his room or playing with his model airplanes. The question sends me flipping through the pre-me photo albums. My parents' wedding photo. My brother in his cowboy boots. My father holding a cat I never met. I don't notice that the photos don't go very far back in time. I focus on my slender mother, no sign of me in her belly. And then, presto digito, there she is sitting in a chair with a swaddled me in her arms. Hmmm…

Later, when I'm brushing my teeth, my father comes into the bathroom. He's going to read me a story. He stands there behind me, waiting patiently, *Jungle Book* in his hand. I look at his eyes. Same watery blue as mine. His hair, also blond, a little darker and sparser. I don't look like my mother, but I sure look like him. Through him, I see myself for the first time. In response to my questions a few days later, my mother tells me she got so big during her pregnancy with me, the doctor thought she was carrying twins. I take this information as proof I'm her birth daughter. "Born in May, you're a Gemini," she says. "*Zwillinge* in German." Of course I am, me and my twin reflection.

When I'm twelve, I ask for a mirror of my own. In my bedroom. I've become very interested in observing myself. I now know this has much to do with the devastating moment, for which I'm totally unprepared, in the YWCA bathroom after swimming class. Inside the brick building on Dorchester, a week before I get my own mirror, I'm squatting in a cubicle inside the ladies' room. I don't feel well. No, that's an understatement. I feel as if a razor blade is scraping the insides of my lower abdomen. I stand to pull my wet Speedo up, see the toilet bowl full of blood. I try to staunch the bleeding with wads of toilet paper that quickly get pink and mushy. I'm in there a long time, and when I come out, I see myself in the mirror. Ghostly pallor, wet hair stuck to my head, terrified face. When I get home, I tell my mother. She is moved for some reason. Explains everything. Gives me a box of pads, two aspirin, and as much ginger ale as I want.

My mirror is long, rather narrow, with a teak frame. It's liberating not to have to wait for the bathroom to be free or sneak into my parents' bedroom. I'm more careful when I get ready for school. Check the hair, the shirt, the butt, hold a hand mirror, turn around. Practise my dance moves. Try not to look as awkward as I feel.

I'm being observed. I know because, one day, my mother says, "You know, when I was growing up, it was considered bad form to spend too much time looking at yourself in the mirror."

I'm blushing but I don't yet recognize shame. I ask her why.

"Because we weren't supposed to care much about how we look."

"You care about what you look like."

"Of course! But, when I was growing up, I was expected to be modest. It was considered a virtue." Then she mentions her mother, who died before I was born. "Your grandmother was very virtuous," she says, and her green eyes ripple, not with happiness but as if stones are being dropped into her core. I've made her sad with all my mirror-gazing, but guilt doesn't stop me. I'm just more careful to shut my bedroom door.

A year later, after the apple trees in our garden have shed their blossoms, I come home from the library with a copy of *Rosemary's Baby* hidden in my bag. I've heard about the movie, but it's rated over eighteen. I'm taking the stairs up to my room when my mother calls me into my parents' bedroom. She's sitting on the side of her bed. On her night table, a stack of books, including the intriguing cover of Germaine Greer's *The Female Eunuch*. But that's not what she wants to show me. An elderly aunt in Europe has mailed an envelope of photos from my mother's childhood. I already know these are cherished since so many family photographs were lost in the flight from Estonia. Sitting next to my mother on the bed, I look at the small black-and-white photos. Nobody's smiling, not even the kids. On top of not looking at yourself in the mirror, you're not supposed to smile at the camera. The Stoics, or maybe it's the Prussians influenced by the Victorian age extending all the way to Estonia and the Russian Empire.

What does it mean to be virtuous? My grandmother is held as the gold standard. Be kind, think of others, turn the other cheek, be humble and honest, have faith, act with charity, share with others, be giving. If called upon, give your life.

In the photographs from Tallinn, my grandmother is dressed simply in a pale linen jacket over a matching knee-length pencil skirt. She has dark hair like my mother's, a sculpted head, and a long neck featuring a necklace of freshwater pearls that I will inherit but never wear. I don't look like her at all.

Yet I carry her name. Between Cora and Siré, she is there. Margarethe.

When I'm twenty-seven, I will travel to Montevideo. I'll find my name engraved on her tomb. Margarethe. Bright sunlight will cast my shadow across her grave, and in this moment, I'll think about how the family called her Gretchen.

IN GRADE NINE, I switch schools and become even more of an outsider. Donnie leaves school to work on a farm. Every day, when I walk to my locker alone, boys make fun of my flat chest. I try to blend in, but I don't understand how I'm perceived. I take dance classes three times a week, piano lessons, and diving, sometimes even batik and painting classes. I'm kept busy so as to stay out of trouble. It takes me too long to realize how most of the kids in my class don't get lessons of any kind. Sometimes I sneak a cigarette out behind the school. Watch the boys on the football and rugby teams run laps around the field.

By the time I'm fourteen, I've made a friend or two in high school. We go to the mall, drink apple cider in the bathroom, and sing "Walk on the Wild Side" on the bus. At home, I listen to stories about dead relatives who, with each telling, become a little more vivid in my imagination.

The summer after grade nine, I travel to Europe with my mother. We visit a riverside café in Hamburg, where a violinist plays Kurt Weill songs on a little stage and we each get to pick a piece of cake from a vast assortment displayed in a long glassed-in counter. The slice is served on a porcelain plate by a white-gloved waiter. My mother and I sit alongside a window with rippling red curtains parted to the view of the river.

"Your grandmother set fire to these curtains once," my mother says. "She was sitting here, dressed in her flapper attire in the 1920s, and gestured with her cigarette holder. The ember ignited the curtains. What a scandal!"

This factoid, that Gretchen smoked, shocks me. It's the first time anything remotely critical has come up around my grandmother. Later, I find out that she used to navigate her 1925 Model-T Ford through the cobblestone streets of Tallinn with more speed than warranted, scaring the horses clip-clopping alongside the earliest cars. Gretchen and her car wound up stuck in a ditch more than once.

I'm learning to drive myself at this point, practising in my parents' white Plymouth Valiant. My father says that, back in Estonia, you didn't need a driver's licence. If you were wealthy enough to buy a car and have it shipped over from Finland, that's all the licence you needed. I'm astonished. My father laughs. Nobody in his family ever had a car in Estonia. He's referring to my mother's family. It must have been entertaining for him to see all the rich people get stuck in ditches, run out of gas on their way home from parties, or dent one another's cars in the winter snow.

It's always like that: my grandmother is rarely discussed. A friend of my mother's gives me a nineteenth-century book of sheet music with songs by Schubert. When I first play the *lieder* on the piano, my mother says, "Your grandmother played the very same songs on the piano in our house in Estonia."

"Which one?" I ask, reading her the titles of songs and playing the opening bars. "Loneliness." "Looking Back." "In Praise of Tears."

"I'm not sure," my mother says. I can tell she's distraught so I don't push her. It's a recurring pattern that frustrates me. Some precision around Gretchen is followed by a vague evasion. But, eventually, a portrait of my grandmother emerges, incomplete and collage-like.

The daughter of a pastor, a serious girl with many sisters and a brother, Gretchen was born, in 1897, to a world totally unlike mine. Estonia was dominated by German landowners and aristocrats and was still part of Tsarist Russia. Since the time of Peter the Great, the Baltic region was considered strategic, a gateway to the West. Tallinn was only a two-hour ferry ride from Finland. For centuries, Estonia had been occupied by a succession of invading forces from Denmark, Germany, Russia, Sweden, and Poland.

Gretchen grew up during the First World War and the Russian Revolution. She witnessed Estonian liberation. Through it all, she played piano, went to school, and at the age of twenty-five, reluctantly married a man whose prosperous family selected her because she was the perfect counterpoint to their wayward son. Her new husband was a man prone to practical jokes, who preferred playing tennis and sailing on the Baltic Sea to studying or working. For their honeymoon, the groom's family paid for a cruise around the world, which is how Gretchen first visited the Americas.

I don't know at what point she realized that her marriage was doomed and that she and her husband were completely mismatched. It happened after the birth of her three children—my mother, followed eleven months later by one uncle, and three years later by the other. In a letter dated February 2, 1930, her husband confessed that he was in love with another woman and asked my grandmother to release him from their marriage. Gretchen responded the very same day. "I do not want to stand in the way of your life," she wrote and agreed to file for divorce. She added several stipulations, including this: should he and his new partner get married (which they did), they and any of their offspring were never to come back to Estonia.

It must have been hard for Gretchen, as the daughter of a pastor, to concede defeat and file for divorce. Yet her father-in-law wrote off his own son and left Gretchen his fortune instead. This is the wealth that allowed her to travel, fly her kids over to Finland to see a dentist, invite friends and relatives for epic parties in her garden. Gretchen continued to live in a house on her in-laws' property, near their villa that was later bombed during the Second World War. During those years, she even helped out in the family firm, bringing food and medical supplies to workers who needed assistance.

Gretchen was guided by her faith, her commitment to her family and loyalty to her brother and sisters and to her mother, who lived with her. Her resources could have enabled her to take the kids and leave for Switzerland or the United States in the late thirties, but she remained in Estonia to keep the family together.

Or so my mother reveals in that café overlooking the river when prodded by my questions.

"Why didn't you get out sooner?" I ask, incredulous.

After the 1939 agreement between the Russians and Germans was signed and Estonia was annexed again, it was too late. They all wound up as refugees, along with everyone in the family who survived. My mother made it to Sweden eventually, where she wanted to stay. But, after the war, Gretchen decided to relocate to Rio de Janeiro with what was left of the family money, which was not much. The Americans had seized most of it. Gretchen thought that it would be easier to arrange for a return of their assets if she were living in Brazil. Also the little money they still possessed would go a lot further in Rio. And it would offer a new beginning, she hoped, for the two children who were still alive—my mother and only one of my uncles.

Imagine landing in Rio in 1947, leaving behind the wasteland of a ruined, hungry Europe and installing yourself in a small apartment on the Copacabana. The beaches, the fruit, the music, the parties! For those final three years of her life, before she was murdered, Gretchen worked diligently to corral lawyers in New York to free up her seized assets so she could rescue the rest of her family—her mother, her brother, her sisters, and their children.

GRETCHEN'S GOODNESS, as I begin to understand, is more easily defined by what not to do. Don't lie, cheat, or steal. Don't skip school. Don't be lazy. Don't criticize others behind their backs. Don't be silly. Don't trust strangers. Don't play with matches. Don't sneak around. Don't make a fool out of yourself. Don't giggle. Don't smile too much. Don't look at yourself in the mirror all the time.

I want to do all of those things when I leave home for university, at seventeen. Such liberation! My dorm room at the University of Ottawa has mirrors just for me—a small one over the desk and a large one inside the door of my closet. Stanton Hall is a high-rise full of rooms identical to mine. Or ours, I should say. I have a roommate whose half of the room is exactly like mine—a twin bed, a desk of pale wood with shelving that reaches to the ceiling and separates the room in two. Louise is older, from somewhere near Quebec City. She has a boyfriend, Gaston, who spends a lot of time in our room. We speak French, and Louise loves correcting me.

"*Pardon*," I say, Parisian-style, when I barge in on the two of them sitting on the bed together.

"*Je m'excuse*," she reminds me.

I open my closet, pull out my clothes for the night, change quickly, and sit at my desk, where I comb my hair while looking in the mirror. I stick my tongue out at myself. I hear Gaston laugh, and it sounds mocking. Turning my head, I see his reflection in the mirror of my open closet door, watching me from his perch on Louise's bed.

Busted. I'm so mortified, I don't even get up to close the door. I always blush easily, and now I'm burning red. Feign indifference, I tell myself, opening my Norton Anthology to *The Canterbury Tales*. I'm very interested in the Wife of Bath and her gapped teeth. A symbol of lust, the professor said. I peek at the reflection in the mirror from my closet door, where Gaston is kissing Louise. I crane my neck to look into the mirror over my desk, studying my teeth. No gaps. I try to go back to my Chaucer. After a few minutes, I get up to close my closet door, Janis Joplin playing in my head—*Freedom's just another word for nothing left to lose*—and I flee the room.

Every Thursday night, there's a party on the ground-floor common area between the women's and men's dorms. Cheap pitchers of beer, nonstop music. I always wear the same thing, a faded blue cowboy shirt with snaps and a long denim skirt. There are small round tables circling a large dance floor. The music is seventies rock. I sit with the girls from my floor. Most of them are nineteen or twenty and grew up in small town Ontario. True-blue Canadians. Like most of the kids I played with on my street growing up, their family histories had more to do with the Depression and maybe the war overseas. They don't know anything about changing countries, immigrants, or refugees. Or blended families that speak various languages. They know nothing about me aside from my inability to cook, which has become a running joke after they catch me eating canned smoked oysters and instant rice for dinner. Plus the fact that my mother calls me every day on the communal phone line. They buy my beer because I'd get carded. The night is long. I love it. Especially toward midnight, when the lights dim down and the mirror ball revolves over the dance floor to "Stairway to Heaven." Some guy I've never seen before asks me to dance. The beer has my head spinning. We stand there swaying, almost clinging to each other. It's a nasty world outside. But, in this moment, I look up at the mirror and see my miniscule blue self in the arms of a boy. *There's a lady who's sure all that glitters is gold…* I want to be her.

NOTHING BRINGS home your own mortality faster than seeing your name on a grave. It's like looking into a mirror and seeing nothing.

I'm in a city I've never visited before. In 1984, Uruguay is still a military dictatorship. In the cab on the way to the Cementerio Britanico, in Montevideo, the driver says there are many other, bigger cemeteries in the city. It's not a great time to be visiting, I'm told. But I've promised my mother I'd visit my grandmother's grave and bring home photographs.

A marble statue of an angel greets me at the entrance to the cemetery. In a gesture of mercy, she embraces two small, sorrowful figures leaning into her. Facing this past, she seems to tells me, will be okay. Have faith.

A labyrinth of alleyways winds past graves, mausolea, and *glorietas*. I walk in the shade of cypress and palm trees. The cemetery feels vast. It's just after noon and the cottage housing the offices is closed. My mother has given me vague directions to the grave site. I scan the names on the tombs, up and down the alleys, through the arbours, past flowerbeds and fountains. Looking for my grandmother's grave in this cemetery involves navigating an unknown world. She lived on this continent for only a few years, as did my mother. This world here is beautiful and lush, as it must have first felt after postwar Europe. It also feels dangerous. Lives were lost here, including Gretchen's.

Beyond a mass of tangled rosebushes, a groundskeeper pushes a wheelbarrow down a path. When I catch up to him, he puts the wheelbarrow down and regards me with some caution. Later, I think about what it must be like to work in a cemetery. All the grief and distraught mourners to contend with, and the graves to dig. But also the beauty of the setting, how in the midst of a city like this one, it is so quiet you can hear the earthly details of bees and sparrows, the skittering of *carpinchos* on the grass. This groundskeeper, an older man in overalls and worn boots, pushes his hat back on his forehead and leans in to decipher my accented Spanish when I tell him I'm looking for my grandmother's grave and mention her name.

"When was the burial?" he asks.

"August 1950."

"A foreigner?"

"Yes, born in Europe."

"Her age?"

"She died at fifty-three."

"How did she die?"

"She was murdered."

After a moment, he nods. "There are two graves from that time. Relatives buried in separate locations. I remember."

He leads me to my grandmother's grave, then retreats. The tomb is dark-grey stone overgrown with three decades of spider plants. There, I discover my middle name etched into the stone. Margarethe.

A SHORT WALK from the cemetery, in the riverside barrio known as Pocitos, Gretchen sits in the room she's temporarily renting. The room is part of a larger apartment owned by a widow. She drinks coffee while reading her small book of psalms. It's early morning. Perhaps she lights a cigarette after opening the window a crack to let in some late-winter air, the sounds of *horneros* chirping in the trees. She hears a knock at her door. There's a man outside. Gretchen knows him well.

"Let me get changed," she says, aware that he's distraught. "Come back in fifteen minutes."

When the man returns, he enters her room and locks the door. The other women in the apartment will later tell police that they heard words being exchanged. Then, at 9:45 a.m., three shots are fired from a Browning pistol. The first two hit Gretchen's breast. With the third, the man shoots himself in the head.

Newspaper accounts of the tragedy say that the landlord and a guard break down the door. Gretchen is already dead, but an ambulance rushes the man to the hospital. After an unsuccessful surgery, he dies a few hours later.

Gretchen's body is prepared for burial in the room where she was murdered. Candles are lit for the vigil, while my mother navigates burial preparations with the help of friends. She is only twenty-seven years old at the time and has been living on her own, in a house in Montevideo, for two years. She notifies her brother in Rio, who sends the family in Europe a telegram. "Deeply shaken. Must share sad news. Our mother died yesterday in Montevideo. Please inform close friends." He does not arrive in time for the interment, two days later.

After burying Gretchen, my mother takes to her bed, sick with grief.

THERE'S A COST to setting down the words of my grandmother's murder. To trying to imagine how it impacted my mother and the rest of Gretchen's descendants, including me. This is the first time I've been able to write about it.

My mother's deep well of sadness did not suffocate her. She refused to live in the past, to be lodged in a tragic narrative. My mother told me the truth, but she also made it understood that this was not a story to be shared outside the family. This shroud of silence hangs over me always. Maybe only I can see it, but it's there. Every time I meet someone who knew or interacted with my family in the past, I wonder. Do they know? And, if they do, how much?

Of the man who knocked at Gretchen's door, I will say only that he was a relative, a person whom Gretchen loved. Someone who lived through the wartime traumas of Europe and was tormented by them.

In a long letter to Gretchen's mother, three weeks after the death, my mother tries to find the words to comfort her grandmother. "What has happened here, this dark, difficult trial, has brought [Gretchen's] deep, selfless love into perspective, a love that I so often disregarded and stepped on. When I was told the terrible news, I had a single hope that I would still see her alive in order to thank her. I now realize this was a selfish impulse. Both bullets killed her on the spot and she did not suffer more..."

In her letters to Europe, my mother emphasizes the beauty of the cemetery, a place where Gretchen had often walked—the cypresses, pines, and flowering apple trees; the many mourners who leave bouquets on Gretchen's grave; and the consolation she finds in knowing that her mother lies peacefully in a beautiful place. As if trying to convince herself, along with everyone else in the family, that some beauty can be dredged from the horror.

# WHAT PEACHES & WHAT PENUMBRAS!

AUNT BETTY was the only adult in my family who didn't speak English with an embarrassing accent. She looked like a movie star, lounging on our back porch as if poolside at The Beverly Hills Hotel. The neighbourhood kids would spy on her through gaps in our cedar hedge.

The year after her divorce and the bankruptcy, Aunt Betty had phoned from Los Angeles. "I deserve a break," she said. "I hear Expo 67 is *the* place to be this summer!"

The day before flying in, Aunt Betty called and told my mother, who was really her cousin several times removed, that she'd be wearing a fake-leopard-skin coat "so you can spot me at the airport."

I whispered to my mother while she was on the phone. "Ask Aunt Betty to bring as many M&M's as possible." At the time, M&M's (*Melts in your mouth, not in your hand!*) weren't available in Canada.

On the Saturday of her arrival, my father changed into a suit and polished his black lace-ups on the porch while I built castles in the backyard sandbox, making myself scarce until my mother called me inside to squeeze into my flowery birthday dress and too-tight party shoes. She changed into a sapphire blue dress that chafed when she hugged me. Before leaving for the airport, we picked a bouquet of hot-pink peonies to present to Aunt Betty.

My father backed the Valiant out of the driveway and onto the street, where four of the neighbourhood kids were playing with Superballs. The kids stepped back and watched us drive past. I knew that look in their eyes. What's the weird immigrant family up to now? I ducked down in the back seat, blushing for our overly fancy outfits.

We got to Dorval Airport early, parking in a lot far from the terminal. The sun was boiling, and I started limping. Once inside, I eyed the cafeteria, remembering their sugar pies, but my mother was in a no-nonsense mood. We sat in Arrivals, waiting for TWA from LAX to land.

After an endless wait during which my parents tried to explain the convoluted story of how I was related to Aunt Betty, passengers began to surge through the glass doors. We got up and pushed to the front of the crowd, on high alert for a fake-leopard-skin coat. My father hoisted me in his arms. I spotted her right away.

Slim and tall with long blond hair, wearing sunglasses so big they almost covered her bangs, my aunt was pulling a suitcase in one hand while holding a giant stuffed purple cow in a headlock under her other arm. I knew instantly that the cow was for me. I also knew, from my mother's stony expression, that she was not impressed. The kitschy cow with its inflated red lips and long eyelashes, a real bell tied by a pink ribbon around its neck, did not meet Mama's high standards around good taste and the educational value of toys.

Before Aunt Betty was allowed to pass through the doors, a man in a uniform took her aside. She stepped back, clutching the cow, which I noticed had horns and an udder. Insisting, the man gently removed the cow from her grip. After a long discussion, she was allowed to proceed into the terminal sans cow. My mother embraced her, my father kissed her hand, and I presented her with the peonies.

"Peachy," Aunt Betty said.

"They're pink."

"I meant you, kid," she said. "Sweet of you, except for the ants."

I thought she was cracking a joke about aunts and ants. But then I spotted critters crawling inside the blooms.

On the drive home, before cocktails on the back porch, Aunt Betty said, "They confiscated the cow. Customs wanted to make sure it didn't contain anything illegal."

"Like M&M's?" I asked.

"Heroin, kid," she said, laughing out loud at my ignorance.

I didn't have the nerve to ask her what heroin was, but on the Monday after Aunt Betty's arrival, the purple cow was delivered to our house by taxi. In the search for drugs, one seam in the cow's underbelly had been cut open and resewn with black thread in loopy stitching.

A FEW YEARS after her visit, my parents announced that they were leaving on a trip to California without me. My brother was away in college, as he was for most of the late sixties, and I had to sleep at the neighbour's for two whole weeks so as not to miss any school. I was only in grade three by then.

My mother promised to call me with blow-by-blows of her visit with Aunt Betty. Reluctantly, I made a card and wrote a few words. *Dear Aunt Betty, How are you? I am sort of fine. Just wish we could see L.A. too. Love, me & the purple cow that you call It.* I was so mad I could barely say goodbye when my parents departed for the airport.

Perhaps because she didn't want to make me feel worse, during our phone calls over the next two weeks, my mother downplayed her accounts of their visit with Aunt Betty. My parents didn't sleep at her house but stayed at a motel with a pool, which made me mad all over again. Aunt Betty lived in a bungalow with her sons. Her ex, Roy, was in and out of the picture. "They still date," my mother said, which I found fabulously interesting.

I'd seen Roy in photos sent along with Aunt Betty's annual Christmas card. He was dashing and tanned, his dark hair slicked back with just a hint of brilliantine. The boys were my brother's age, late teens, and as blond as Aunt Betty. After the bankruptcy of the family business, Roy never came through with much in the way of child support. Aunt Betty raised her sons on her own, scraping by on quick money after she'd spent her inheritance.

Just as my parents had started to establish themselves, I later learned, things went downhill for Aunt Betty. Which was maybe the reason my parents decided to pay her a visit that spring. Duty and gratitude were among my mother's guiding principles. What I do know is that Aunt Betty resolutely refused to succumb to a more modest lifestyle. Arriving at her bungalow, my parents found her outside, dressed in a floral house dress, matching turban, and sunglasses, commandeering a dump truck, a forklift, and a crew of workers. Her sons, Howie and Dieter, sat on the front steps while their lawn was being ripped out and replaced with massive mounds of pink sand, later smoothed by a paver. The contractors worked all day while my parents drank Aunt Betty's iced tea (terribly sweet, my mother told me, and made with some powder like Tang—I was so jealous). It was late afternoon by the time the work was finished. My parents were hungry and suggested going out for a meal. Aunt Betty refused to leave until the birds arrived. For the upgrade to her house, she'd ordered a flock of plastic flamingos to plant in the pink sand.

MY MOTHER's loyalty to her cousin had more to do with Aunt Betty's parents, Irma and Fritz, who in 1954 drove their big boat of a car 2,700 miles across America to attend her and my father's wedding.

"Was Aunt Betty there?" I asked when my mother told me stories about their wedding day.

Aunt Betty missed my parents' big day. Months earlier, she'd impulsively married Roy in Tijuana, the same place where, impulsively, they later got divorced. Fritz employed Roy at his airplane-parts business. For my parents' wedding, Roy had to mind the business while Fritz and Irma drove from California to Pennsylvania.

Irma and Fritz stopped at diners and Howard Johnsons, making it to Bryn Mawr on the morning of the wedding.

Their pink Cadillac with its tail fins, chrome fenders, and louvers stood out in the simple austerity of Quaker country. Aside from my brother, they were the only family members to attend the low-key afternoon ceremony. The rest of the guests were friends my mother had made while studying at the local college.

A scholarship student on a soon-to-expire visa, she'd just graduated magna cum laude with a master's in Spanish literature and, she later told me, married my father with great reluctance. Her dream was to teach college, pursue a doctorate, and lead an academic life.

In the wedding photo, my mother is wearing a white suit adorned with a corsage of white gardenias. She's staring into the camera, a resigned smile on her lips. Maybe she was wondering how they'd ever build a life together. Or, having been married before, maybe she was thinking that she should have known better. My father looks deliriously happy despite all the obstacles he'd endured since arriving in Canada from Europe with nothing but his violin.

Irma and Fritz contributed the champagne for the wedding reception, held in my mother's studio apartment. Since my mother couldn't cook, my father had prepared the food with an overreliance on the good old Eastern European staple: beets. "Everything was pink!" my mother told me. "The salads, the sour cream, even the little sandwiches."

During the party, Fritz took my father aside and offered him a job at his business, in LA.

"How could he have turned it down?" I asked my mother, convinced that my life would have been so much better in California.

"Thank God he said no!" she responded. "What about the Vietnam War? Your brother might have been drafted if we became Americans."

I'm not sure whether my parents got to spend their wedding night alone together. Who would've looked after my brother, who was already five years old by then? They wound up postponing their honeymoon until after they'd settled in Montréal and saved some money for a trip to Italy. From even before I knew the meaning of the verb, I'd been told I was *conceived* on a Venetian gondola.

In any case, shortly after the wedding, Irma and Fritz got into their Cadillac for the forty-hour drive home. My father tied a white gardenia to their radio antenna for good luck.


Aunt Betty's father was a true believer in the American dream. Born in 1888, Fritz couldn't wait to leave Europe. When he was sixteen, his wanderlust compelled him to sneak aboard a ship docked in a port, most likely Rotterdam.

Fritz travelled as a stowaway and eventually made his way to California. When he got there, he found a job on the assembly line of an airplane factory, an experience he eventually parlayed into a business of his own, supplying the Lockheed Aircraft Company, in Burbank, with small parts manufactured in his shop.

It took me years to grasp the convoluted story of how I was related to Aunt Betty. Among Fritz's siblings, there's a brother, one Emil Fahle, who was my mother's grandfather. He, too, was an entrepreneur and, some said, an opportunist. Emil married into an Estonian family with money, which he used to build a business that stretched to Canada and the US, assets the Americans later seized during the war.

Emil died before the Second World War, before his family and offspring were forced to leave Estonia. His villa in Tallinn was destroyed by German bombs. After the country's independence in the nineties, one of his paper mills was refurbished into a glass high-rise, which was designed to perch on top of the original factory. On the ground floor of the so-called Fahle House, there's a café that used to sell Fahle Tiramisu, an odd memoriam considering the Italian speciality was not available in Estonia during Emil's lifetime.

In a sense, Fritz is to the American dream as Emil is to the European nightmare. The Fahle brothers represented two sides of the same record about bust to boom to bust.

Although Aunt Betty was my mother's cousin and the same age, there was a generation between them. Both experienced the rise and fall of family fortunes, the circumstances of being nouveau riche and nouveau pauvre. Yet they were as different as they looked: my mother had green eyes and short black hair while Aunt Betty had blue eyes and long blond hair.

As a kid, what I adored about Aunt Betty was that her easygoing attitude absolved me of my mother's high standards. I only visited her once, but I got the sense that, no matter what happened in her life, Aunt Betty never forgot how to have fun. She outlived my parents by decades. She even outlived one of her sons.

Born in California, Aunt Betty was unilingual and had never lived in a warzone. She loved Hollywood and was guided by the simplistic moralities of the large-studio films. Meanwhile, my mother spoke seven languages and had travelled across Europe, to Brazil and Uruguay and then the US, to finally land in Canada. She immersed herself in books and considered many Hollywood movies to be low-brow, vacuous, and lacking in nuance.

My mother did, however, love some films, and my parents often took us to the movies. We saw *Beckett* when I was about three. I have blurry memories of Peter O'Toole engaged in numerous sword fights between my napping. More vivid is *Death in Venice*, the 1971 Visconti film that my parents took me to see, probably because they couldn't get a babysitter. I was excited about discovering the location where I was *conceived* yet shocked by images like the rivulets of black hair dye running down the obsessed main character's face. I hadn't known that men dyed their hair.

A FEW YEARS later, out of loyalty to Aunt Betty, our family went to see a film featuring her sons' cars. Howie and Dieter had become gearheads. They bought jalopies, vintage automobiles, and hot rods; fixed them up; and rented them out to film studios, fancy weddings, and Hollywood parties. Aunt Betty's Christmas cards named-dropped the stars who were clients of her sons', hinting at her underlying pride. I was so impressed. *American Graffiti*, directed by George Lucas and produced by Francis Ford Coppola, ended up being 1974's surprise box-office hit, grossing over $200 million.

Sitting in the cinema with my ginormous popcorn and ginger ale, I tried to look out for Howie and Dieter's cars. But I got caught up in the story, which was set in 1962 Modesto, California. Instead of noticing the T-Bird, I was hypnotized by the mysterious blonde (played by Suzanne Somers) in the car, who totally resembled Aunt Betty.

We left the cinema a divided family. My father liked the movie for its music while I liked the coming-of-age story, which resonated because I was about to come of age myself. My mother, however, used words like *superficial*, *lacking nuance*, *undeveloped characters*, *sexist*. I was a teenager and didn't possess the vocabulary to argue with her.

Though Aunt Betty dreamed of her sons' fame and fortune, a car fanatic website says that George Lucas paid local gearheads only $25 for their classic cars while making the film. During the shoot, they got to hang around every night, gawking at the actors and drag-racing on the back streets.

Shortly after Howie died, I came across some lines from Allen Ginsberg's "Wild Orphan" that read like a eulogy: *he's the son of the absconded / hot rod angel— / and he imagines cars / and writes them in his dreams...*

M&M'S WERE still unavailable in Canada by the time my parents finally took me to California. But they weren't the reason for our trip. By the time I was fifteen, my obsessions with candy had been replaced by Isadora Duncan, dance, and romance or lack thereof. I was still struggling with my weirdness and desperately wanted someone to say to me, "I love you." And to be able to say it back!

As a reward for getting good marks in grade ten, my parents took me on a trip to the West Coast. We first visited San Francisco, where we passed by Haight-Ashbury with its head shops and psychedelic paraphernalia.

I was especially on the lookout for penumbras. My brother had recently introduced me to the beat poets. When he was home from college, he'd read me Allen Ginsberg. Finding "Howl" with its *angelheaded hipsters* too long for my teenage attention span, I preferred "A Supermarket in California," the poem addressed to Walt Whitman. My brother and I loved the line, *What peaches and what penumbras!* I assumed that penumbras had to be exotic melons available only in California.

In Haight-Ashbury, I saw the City Lights Bookstore, founded by Lawrence Ferlinghetti. I saw dealers on the street, police cruisers on surveillance, shops with crates of fresh peaches and mammoth tomatoes. But I could not find any penumbras. Not even over in Chinatown. My parents were perplexed by my quest for a lowly melon, and I got tired of trying to explain the importance of things hipster to my mother.

A few days later, we flew to LA. I was excited about seeing Aunt Betty again after a decade. We would spend three days with her, including a visit to the original Disneyland, in Anaheim.

We landed at LAX in the early afternoon. Before taking a bus into the city, my parents left me alone with the luggage while they went to the bathrooms. With all the dance and ballet lessons, I'd become skinny. My mother was now preoccupied with getting me to eat. If I look at photos of me from our trip out west, with my long hair about the same colour as Aunt Betty's, I can see that I appeared older than fifteen. So maybe that explains why, during that trip to California, I was a magnet for Jesus freaks, Vietnam War veterans, and strolling minstrels. I was too polite to ignore them, too shy to respond to their entreaties.

Seconds after my parents left me, I was swarmed by a group of Hare Krishna dancers. They played bells and drums, all wearing white, the men with shaved heads, the women, some of them almost my age, with long stringy hair. I sat there pretending they didn't exist, fighting back tears until my parents returned. Wading through the group, my father pulled out coins from his pocket while my mother chatted with the youngest Hare Krishna-ites, praising their commitment to peace.

Aunt Betty treated us to city tours of Beverly Hills and Hollywood. We spent a whole day at Disneyland. She offered to buy me a stuffed unicorn as company for my purple cow. I refused, politely I hope, hurt that she still thought of me as a kid. I considered myself a full-fledged adult, no longer easily seduced by her banter. She seemed to get along really well with my mother, and I started to get jealous. I was astonished at Mama's enthusiasm about some of the inevitable kitsch of Disneyland—the fakery of Sleeping Beauty's Castle and Tomorrowland. She loved It's a Small World After All, the water ride in Fantasyland with the dancing children and the theme of global peace. I found it cheesy and childish and fantasized about telling her the ride was *superficial* or *lacking nuance*. It was the beginning of a long rebellion directed at my mother that lasted until I was twenty-five.

We never got to see Aunt Betty's house. She claimed it was "a mess." My mother whispered that Dieter and Howie had deserted some old cars in the backyard. I was disappointed not to be able to see the pink sand and flamingos firsthand.

On our last day, Aunt Betty hugged me goodbye. "Here's looking at you, kid," she said. I didn't understand the reference, but I did feel a bit sad leaving her, as if sensing I'd never see her again. We got on the shuttle to the airport. From my seat by the window, I watched her sway down the entrance of the hotel into the smog of LA. In her peach sundress and high-heeled shoes, she looked old-fashioned for the seventies, like a starlet from an era before Nixon, the Vietnam War, the emergence of counterculture, hippies, and free love.

The bus stopped at a few other hotels to pick up passengers. Outside The Beverly Wilshire, a guy was standing on the sidewalk. Long dark hair, jeans, a tie-dyed T-shirt, and round wire glasses like John Lennon's. He caught me watching him and mouthed the words: "I love you."

Whenever The Doors played on the radio, Jim Morrison's 1968 song *Hello, I Love You* cracked me up. But, the first time someone declares their love to you, there's nothing funny about it. I always wondered about the guy standing outside my bus window in LA and how he'd loved me for a split second.


M&M's finally arrived in Canada in the eighties. I don't think I ever bought them, my obsession with the candy replaced by studying, working, loving, and all the growing up I had to do. The rudest awakening came when my parents died. I was an adult, but I felt like an orphan anyway. I hadn't stayed in touch with Aunt Betty, but after she sent me a sympathy card, we started to correspond.

Aunt Betty wrote sporadic letters in the loopy, crowded script of a schoolgirl rather than the eighty-year-old she'd become. I tried to answer her letters with factoids and reminiscences I hoped would entertain her. She was living in a seniors' home near LA, not far from her son Dieter. One of my favourite letters arrived in 2008, ten years after my mother's death. It was folded inside an envelope bearing a Greta Garbo stamp and two return addresses, her own and Dieter's, just in case.

> *Dear "niece,"*
>
> *Of course I remember that purple cow. I believe it was called "It," right? I still have the leopard skin coat and get lots of compliments wearing it. I get rave comments from everyone these days as I never seem to age.*
>
> *All very nice, but there is a very bad side to it, too, like outliving your precious children (one dead). All our wonderful husbands are now gone, and some of the wives are going, too. I still have thoughts of finding a husband. Even a boyfriend would be nice, but when a handsome young guy finds you're old enough to be his mom, try grand-ma, all the fun is gone (this has already happened!!!)*
>
> *Sorry this was all about me, me, me!!! Recently I got to talking to our much-loved favorite baritone, Ralph [who told of] his trip to Estonia and how he loved it! So great to hear about the building and café, the Fahle restaurant. How my dad would have loved to hear of this having spent half his life in cafés! Thanks so much for the lovely card and news. Don't work too hard.*
>
> *Love to all, xxxooo Betty.*

I NEVER received word of Aunt Betty's death. An online record of her obituary says only that she "died May 1, 2011, aged 87 years, 4 months, 4 days."

There's a shadow over the question of whether I ever really loved her. My affection might well have been an imaginary product, a California dream shaded by an elaborate reaction to my mother's countenance, like those elusive penumbras.

# RUSALKA

It all starts at the statue of a mermaid who looks like an angel. "Statue was erected in 1902," the guide says, "to mark ninth anniversary of sinking of Russian warship."

The Soviet guide goes by Frau Anna because her last name is so convoluted, nobody in the tour group can get it right.

"Rusalka, or mermaid," she says, "was sculpted by Amandus Adamson."

We're all standing there squinting up at a massive angel brandishing an Orthodox cross. The statue, with her wings and feet, is obviously an angel, not a mermaid. My German's too shabby to ask questions. I wish the tour were in English, then it wouldn't be so hard to concentrate. But there seem to be no other English-speaking tourists in Estonia. The only visitors, aside from me and my mother, are over sixty and European. The sun's boiling even though this place is supposed to be a front in the Cold War.

Em is wearing the floppy hat she tried to foist on me back in the hotel room. I'm too old to call her Mama anymore, so I just call her Em. She thinks Frau Anna is probably a spy. I figured she was exaggerating about all the spying until I saw a man in the hallway outside our room carrying spools of tape. After that, I wondered if she was right about the rooms being bugged.

Most North Americans aren't even allowed here, Em said. "Not behind the Iron Curtain." Which, I found out yesterday, doesn't really exist. When the ferry docked in the port of Tallinn, I'd been expecting to pass through one of those cool stringy curtains with iron ball bearings instead of glass beads.

"Model for mermaid was sculptor's housekeeper, Juliana Rootsi." Frau Anna spits the Estonian name as if she's swearing.

Em stiffens and grabs my wrist. She takes a deep breath. I brace myself.

"*We wait each minute, longing, longing,*" Em whispers. "*For Freedom's sacred fleeting bliss. The way young lovers fret while counting the minutes to a secret tryst.*"

I don't know what's worse, my mother quoting Pushkin or being in this group with every minute of the day preplanned. I'm not even allowed to take photos in certain places, like the port, government buildings, or military installations.

Frau Anna points at the carved plaque on the base of the memorial. It's hard to see from this distance, but it looks like a group of bodies. "Sailors from *Rusalka* warship who perished by drowning," she says. "Carved in bronze, same alloy used for statue."

Who cares? I glance over at Em to see whether she does. But my mother is staring at a spot to the left of the angel. I follow her line of vision and that's when I first see him.

Ankles crossed, he's leaning against the statue. A cigarette dangles from his lips and he's wearing a snappy white top with a rectangular collar and blue piping that matches the colour of his bell-bottom pants. He looks about eighteen, just a few years older than me. His hair is short and sun-bleached, and he's very tanned. I catch my breath. But why is Em staring at the hunk? Typical and so embarrassing.

I wander off to take some photographs of Kadriorg Park with its long *allee* of trees. From a distance, the Rusalka Memorial looks a lot like the angel statue back home, the one by the mountain in the centre of Montréal. It makes me homesick to think of it, my girlfriends and the strip poker games I'll be missing. I try to get Mick Jagger back in my head. *Angie, Angie, when will those clouds all disappear?* Overhead, woolly clouds dance like little sheep in the sky. But I can't hear the song all the FM stations were playing when I left home.

It must have escaped me during the ferry ride from Helsinki, just after Em asked for a cognac. "I need something. Hurry!" So I rushed to the onboard bar and ordered the drink, expecting to be carded. But no, the bartender slid a tumbler toward me, full to the brim, and walking back to Em, I took a sip, coughed, and spilled some of the stuff on my top. I handed her the cognac.

"Way too much!" she admonished, as if it were my fault. Still, she emptied the glass to give her the strength, she said, to face the Soviet border guards waiting on the docks.

Maybe it was the cognac, but there were no tears when Em first spotted Tallinn approaching in the distance. The medieval fairy tale town hovered on a little mound. Em pointed to the spires and landmarks, naming each of them. "Imagine, I left thirty-four years ago and it looks so familiar! In '39, when we left by ship in a hurry, the Estonians stood grim-faced on those docks and watched us leave. Soviet soldiers were about to take over their country."

Em almost cried as the ferry slowed to dock. As soon as we stepped off the gangplank, guards with uniforms and crewcuts demanded our passports. One of them rifled through my suitcase. When it was Em's turn, they confiscated a Finnish newspaper and threw in it in the garbage.

"Come, quickly!" Em calls me over now, as we stand around Rusalka. "We're doing a group photo."

The oldsters gather around the base of the statue. Frau Anna has slung all their cameras around her neck and raises them one by one to snap photos. I stand next to Em in the back row, smiling the I'm-finally-without-braces grin I've been practising in the bathroom mirror. I smell tobacco and turn. The sailor's face is inches away, his eyes black and intense above high cheekbones. He must be from one of the Soviet warships anchored in the port of Tallinn, which Em says are a threatening reminder to the Estonians of who's in charge. I panic.

"Em!" I cry out. My mother turns and laughs, her green eyes shining from under the brim of the floppy hat. Her reaction eggs the sailor on, and he puts his arms around both of us, as if he belongs with these tourists sight-seeing a country they'd been kicked out of decades ago. So much for a mother's protection. I grit my teeth for another photo. He whispers something in Russian and then he's gone.


ALL MORNING and into the afternoon, Frau Anna guides us through the old churches in the city of Tallinn. Just when I can't take another icon, Em grabs my arm and we sneak out the side door into an alleyway and run until we reach a cobblestone square. Em starts looking for a konditorei she remembers from her childhood, which apparently is still in operation. As long as the place has food, I'm thinking, and no Frau Anna.

"I see it!" Em points at a faded awning. There's a line of people snaking from the glass doors into the square. My mother's got that determined walk now that she's found our destination. She goes to the door and it opens immediately. A maître d' waves us inside. Em asks him something in Estonian, but it turns out he's Russian. Em switches languages and asks him the same thing, something about the line of people who have gone silent. They're staring at me and Em.

My mother's eyes go hard and she removes her hat like she's going to use it to whack the maître d'. Em speaks some Russian and then takes my hand. "We're going to line up. With them." The maître d' shrugs and shuts the door.

"It'll take forever! I'm starving. Isn't there somewhere else—"

Em gives me her nonnegotiable look, so I follow her to the end of the line. A few Estonians nod at us.

"Do you understand what happened?" Em asks. "He wanted to let us in because we're tourists. Russians and tourists don't have to line up. The Estonians do."

"That's so unfair! It's their country."

"Exactly."

We stand in the square waiting. The lineup inches forward very slowly and it seems like forever, the definition of which is chemistry class on Friday afternoons. Em starts telling about the rusalka, a female ghost in Slavic mythology. She's a spirit who has to live out her time on earth, with other ghosts. The rusalki live at the bottoms of rivers, and in the middle of the night, they emerge to play in the meadows. If they see handsome men, they fascinate them with songs and dances. "Once they've mesmerized the men," Em says, "they lead them to the river floor and to their death."

"They're not real, are they?"

"I knew some Russians who claimed to have seen them."

"No way."

"Their eyes flicker like green fire, they're extremely pale, and their shiny hair is perpetually wet. A rusalka can't survive on dry land for very long, but she has a magic comb and, with it, she's always safe. The comb gives her the power to conjure water whenever she needs it."

"So they're like mermaids?"

"Mermaid-like. More water nymph or succubus."

"What?"

"*What* is impolite." Em starts explaining that a succubus is a female demon who seduces men, but she stops when an old lady in front of us turns around. She's got a very wrinkled face and startling blue eyes that stare at Em for a long time until she whispers something in Estonian. Em answers and takes my hand for a moment. I know what she's saying because she tells everyone we meet the exact same thing: how she left Estonia, at the age of sixteen, as part of a mass deportation in September 1939, and how she's finally returned to show her daughter, also sixteen, where she was born. The most important things you can give your kids, she often adds, are roots and wings.

But the whispering goes on and I stand there, basically excluded. The lineup surges and we finally get a table in the konditorei. Em orders in Russian and I let her pick whatever. I open my purse and slide out the diary with the little lock my father gave me at the airport in Montréal, making sure Em doesn't see my secret hiding place for the key. Then I rummage for a pen. Aside from a few lists and song lyrics, I haven't written anything since we landed in Finland.

"How do you spell *rusalka*?"

Em's answer seems wrong because the memorial had two *s*'s, as in *russalka*. "Rusalka is the Estonian spelling," she says.

It's so confusing. Every place has three names, Estonian, Russian, and German. They should just stick to one spelling and that should be Estonian. I start writing about the wet hair and the magic comb until the waiter arrives with two bowls of very red broth and some bread. Then he brings glasses of sour milk, the same thin yoghurt we got for breakfast at the hotel.

While we're eating, the wrinkled woman from the lineup passes the table and drops a folded sheet of paper by Em's soup bowl. Em keeps eating with one hand as she slides the paper into a side pocket of the purse on her lap.

"What's that?"

"I'll tell you later."

"Nobody here speaks English, Em. Just tell me."

"I promised to mail a letter for her once we get home."

"Why doesn't she just send it?"

"Censorship. Their letters are opened." Then she says, "I don't mind, you know."

"What? I mean…what's not to mind?"

"You calling me Em." Then she gives me the I-know-you're-going-through-a-phase look.

"It's short for *ema*, which, as you know, is *mother* in

Estonian." I don't tell her the real reason. That I don't want to sound like a child, that I want her to treat me like an adult.

"Finish your soup."

We're sitting alone at a table for four although all the others have been jammed together, sharing tables even if they're just two. The ice creams Em orders make up for the weird broth. I'm licking my spoon when I see him through the glass doors.

"Em! Don't look now but he's here."

Of course Em turns around. I'm blushing so hard my face practically melts my ice cream. Em does exactly the wrong thing and waves the sailor over. I slide my diary into the purse and give her a dirty look.

"*Pozhaluysta*," Em says, pointing to the empty chair, and the sailor sits down.

He orders something in Russian and starts chatting with Em. At first, I can guess what they're saying. His name is Misha, he's from Saint Petersburg, which he calls Leningrad but Em corrects him. At one point, I realize Em is telling the I-was-sixteen-and-she's-sixteen story because Misha ogles me and nods. Em's Russian seems to improve with every sentence, and soon they're laughing at whatever. Then Misha jumps up and goes to the counter.

"What's he doing?"

"He's treating us to champagne."

"It's late. We should be getting back to the hotel."

"For what? Who's waiting for us?"

"*What* is impolite. I hate the Russians and I hate him too."

"Your father's parents were born in Russia. It's like hating yourself." Em gives me the how-ignorant-you-are look.

Misha comes back with the waiter, who brings a bottle

of champagne and three flutes on a silver tray. This is going nowhere fast.

I clink my glass with Em's and Misha's. The stuff tastes sour, nothing like the ginger ale that it looks like. Misha and Em are talking and laughing. My mother's probably telling him about her convoluted past and mixed-up origins, part Estonian, Russian, and Baltic German, because he looks at me, nods, and says "*Da*" and something else that Em translates as, "She looks Estonian with her blue eyes and fair hair." He talks some more and Em nods, "Like an angel, you are right."

Then he focuses back on Em and I try to figure out what exactly he sees in my mother. After her second champagne, Em's green eyes glitter beneath the long black eyelashes I've always wanted. It must be the drinks because she doesn't really look like my mother. As if who my mother is and where she belongs can change depending on where she is and whom she's hanging out with. My mother has always struggled with what she calls "the trappings of domesticity," especially when she's cooking dinner and she'd rather be reading poetry.

Misha takes my mother's hand and turns up the palm, as if reading her future. "*Ty takaya krasivaya.*" Em giggles.

"What did he just say?"

"You are so beautiful."

This is getting way out of hand. I can't figure out how to end it without making a scene. Just as I'm about to fake stomach cramps, Misha jumps up, rushes to the counter, and pays.

"He has to be back on the ship soon," Em says. "What a shame!"

"Are you drunk?"

"Let's go," she says quietly.

I know I've insulted her but I think she deserves it. My father would feel sad at her flirting.

It's PAST TEN and getting dusky, and the streetlights are too weak to make much of a difference. The cobblestone square seems quaint and mysterious. Two old men are sitting on the sidewalk sharing a bagged bottle. One of them starts singing in Estonian.

When Misha comes out of the konditorei, he says something to Em. She shakes her head, so he shrugs. All of a sudden, he grabs my hand and bows to kiss it. No guy has ever kissed my hand before. My lips, yes, my neck, definitely, but never my hand. He does the exact same thing to Em and then saunters off toward the port.

"What did he just say?"

"He offered to walk us back to the hotel."

"Not a good idea."

"I know."

Em's sense of direction is lousy even at home, so she lets me lead the way. It's pretty easy to locate the Intourist Hotel with its red neon sign on the roof of the highest building in Tallinn. I keep looking up at it as I guide us through the crooked alleys and dark streets.

Just when we're a block from the hotel, a police van pulls up ahead of us. Two men get out, bang on a door, and disappear into the house. Em and I stand there, frozen like two statues. In seconds, the men come back out, dragging a man in his pyjamas.

Em shrieks, starts running, and trips on the cobblestones.

I sprint to grab her arm and pull her up. The police throw the man in the back of the van and drive off.

"What just happened?"

"Another Estonian." Em is panting. "*Abgeschleppt*...to the gulag."

"Where's that?"

"Far away. Siberia. Prison. Labour camps."

My stomach cramps up for real. How can they just take someone away like that? Em holds on to my arm for the rest of the walk.

When we enter the hotel, Frau Anna ambushes us in the lobby and starts berating Em in German. The hotel is like a prison. When we checked in, yesterday afternoon, we had to hand in our passports at the reception desk. What if Frau Anna reports us? Em manages to get rid of her and we take the elevator up to the sixth floor.

"I need a shower," Em says. She goes into the bathroom and shuts the door.

I change into my T-shirt and sweatpants, brush my hair, and lie down on the bed. I'm too tired to write in the diary. I think of my father. "Promise you'll call me the minute you arrive back in Helsinki," he said at the airport. "Let me know your mother's safe." My parents think that, just because I was born in Canada, nothing can happen to me here. Frau Anna could get us thrown into a police van and we wouldn't even have our passports to prove we're Canadians.

Em comes out of the bathroom wrapped in a skimpy towel that barely covers her full breasts and pubic hair. She's holding a comb. "My hair is so full of knots—help me."

Em sits on the edge of the bed and I, cross-legged behind

her, gently pull the comb through the wet hair. It smells chalky, like Soviet soap. Her shoulders are round, her neck long, and her back is very straight, the smooth amber skin shiny with droplets of water. Even though she's exactly fifty, she seems younger without her clothes on. No wonder Misha was mesmerized.

"What did Misha say to you?"

"A sweet boy. He knows his Pushkin."

"He quoted poetry?" Of course that's the key to unlocking Em's heart. "He really liked you."

"Truth is, he was after you, my daughter."

"No way."

"Everywhere we go together, the men are looking at you."

They are? I keep combing. If I could see her green eyes, I'd know for sure whether she's jealous of me. How could she be? I'm her daughter. She said it herself.

Beyond my mother's head, the lights of the warships flicker in the port. "You think Estonians will ever be free?"

"I may not live to see it," Em whispers, "but you will."

"How do you know?"

Em shivers for a second. She gets up to put on her nightie, then reaches for my hand and pulls me into the bathroom. She shuts the door and turns on the water in the sink. I sit beside her on the edge of the bathtub. Em says, "I don't want them to hear me saying this, but you need to know. How courageous the Estonians are."

I'm freaking out. Maybe the bathroom's bugged too. Whatever Em's about to say, it's something that could get us into trouble.

"Every time they gather for their song festivals, they

stand together and sing their national anthem. Even though it's outlawed. Even though the Soviet military is sitting there, armed and in uniform. The Estonians stand up and sing. That's why I think one day they will sing their way to freedom. I might be dead by then, but you could witness it." Em gets up and starts brushing her teeth.

I leave the bathroom and go to the window. What if Misha is waving from the deck of a distant warship? *Angie, you're beautiful, / but ain't it time we said goodbye?* What if he's been mesmerized? He'll end up drowning. The thought makes me feel queasy. *Let me whisper in your ear, Angie, Angie / Where will it lead us from here?*

Em was right about the Estonians and what came to be known as their singing revolution. A few years after we buried my father, Boris Yeltsin climbed onto a tank in Moscow, in August 1991, and convinced the military to defect. Em binge-watched newscasts of Estonians taking over media outlets, calling on people to act as human shields to defend the television and radio stations from Soviet tanks. When Estonia declared independence, two days later, Em requested a glass of cognac. We never spoke of Misha again. But I always wondered about my mother's magic comb and her ability to mesmerize men.

# THE MARK

VIRGILIA JUMPS the fence and takes the stairs down to the ice. Snow is falling in the dusky sky. Somewhere behind Parliament Hill, the sun is setting. A few disconcerting cracks as she tiptoes across the Rideau Canal, a dangerous undertaking before it's officially open to skaters. Every January, there are reports of people falling through thin ice. The canal isn't deep, but the prospect of sinking into a black hole of frigid water and being photo-shamed in a newspaper makes every footstep a thrilling wager.

After she crosses the canal, her next gamble has to do with where to sit in Pigeon Bleu once she gets there. She follows the footpath along Colonel By Drive, a twenty-minute walk through slush that seeps into her leaky left boot.

The bar is dark with a few overhead lights and a song playing on the sound system, Hall and Oates by the sound of it. Pamela is singing along while she dries glasses behind the wooden counter. *It's a bitch girl, but it's gone too far...* It's early enough that just a few tables are taken: a group of students, some civil servants stopping for drinks on the way home from work. The latter are Virgilia's target. They have money to blow, and she doesn't like to further impoverish someone scraping through school. Her lucky booth is empty, and even though sitting at a table is likely to bring her more business, Virgilia slides in.

Pamela comes over, singing, her long hair swinging down to her butt. "*Say money but it won't get you too far…* How were your holidays?"

"Good, but I'm glad to be back in Ottawa."

"Missed us? Ha! We're happy you're back. Good for business." She looks around. "I think you'll be lucky today. Did school start?"

"Last week. It's my final semester and I've got a full load." Virgilia says this knowing exactly what Pamela's going to say next.

"Study hard. Don't drop out like I did."

"You could still go back."

"I knew you'd say that!" Her bracelets jangle as she wipes down the table. "Ben is in the back making sandwiches. But he might come out for a game later."

After ordering her usual hot milk and biscotti, Virgilia kicks off her boots so her sock will dry by the time she heads home. Then she sets up one of the backgammon boards Ben leaves for customers on various tables. He's the one who taught her how to play for money.

Soon enough, some guy approaches the booth and sits down across from her. Sliding across the cracked vinyl upholstery, his pants snag. Perfect. She doesn't want him to get too comfortable. He loosens his tie and places a dollar bill on the table.

"Here you go."

"Thanks."

She must have played him before, but she doesn't remember his face. It's nondescript, as anyone over forty strikes her. A moustache, pug nose, sad eyes. She stares into those eyes to distract him. He rolls the dice and makes his moves. She beats him handily and takes the dollar bill. He wavers, then reaches for the wallet in his blazer and places another dollar bill on the table. "One last kick at the can."

Virgilia beats him in a few moves.

"You're not cheating, are you?"

"Of course not."

"How come you never lose?"

"Practice."

He slides out of the booth and joins his friends at their table. They look toward her as he loosens his tie, shaking his head.

It still amazes Virgilia how easy it is to win at backgammon. The game is part skill and strategy, part luck. After playing daily with her roommate in first year, she memorized pretty well every permutation and combination. By second year, after a few sessions with Ben, she was earning about twenty dollars a week at Pigeon Bleu. Enough for groceries and a few extras. The regulars who come to drink beers on their way home from government work are the easiest opponents. Their knowledge of the game is so shallow, they don't even get basic probabilities. For instance, when rolling the dice, the most likely result—almost 20 percent—is a total of seven. Plus the drinking makes their thinking wobbly and their moves overly confident.

Sometimes the men, since there are hardly any women in the place, hit on her, but that's rare. Pamela and Ben keep an eye on things, won't hesitate to come over and tell the guy to leave Virgilia alone. Generally, though, few guys are interested in a girl who can beat them at a simple game. Being good at backgammon makes her feel protected.

The place is starting to fill up. Another man in a suit plays her twice and, again, she beats him handily, pleased with the elegance of her strategy, the swift movement of her hands on the board. He's too impulsive and doesn't take the time to think things through. She knows she should leave considering she's four bucks in, but Virgilia is on a winning streak and the players keep coming.

Sometime around eight, a blast of cold air from the open door lets in a tall man in jeans with two women. They sit at the bar and order a round of beers. Virgilia recognizes the man, not so much from his looks but from his checked flannel shirt and hunched shoulders. Like he's carrying a heavy knapsack. She's careful to keep her head turned, let her long hair fall over her face. Sometimes, not looking at someone who's used to people looking at him makes him notice. Maybe that's why he gets up from the stool and walks to her booth.

"I know you," he says. "You're in one of my classes. Which one?"

"Mondays and Wednesdays, three to five."

"Ah, yes. CanPo. The semester's still young." He laughs. "What's your name?"

"Virgilia."

"Mind if I call you Virge?"

"Yes." She means *yes, I mind*, but he doesn't get it.

"So Virge, the bartender says you're here a lot. That you're the best player in Ottawa. How about we play a game?"

"I was just about to leave."

Professor Nave sits down anyway. Slides and gets snagged on the ripped vinyl. "What are the stakes?" His legs are so long they brush her knees. She angles herself sideways.

"A dollar a game." Normally, she makes sure her opponent places the bill on the table up front. That way, if they don't have change, they'll get it from Pamela before the game starts. But she decides to trust the professor.

"So who goes first, Virge?"

"You do."

"What if I want to go second?"

"Then I'll go first."

He rolls the dice. Double ones. "Ah well. Not a good start, is it?"

"You get to roll again."

His game goes downhill from there. "Let's play one more. I'll win back my buck."

"Maybe."

"Have you ever read *The Gambler*?"

"No."

He loses again, sighs, and gives her a two-dollar bill. "The bartender was right. But you know how it is, Virge? Lucky in backgammon, unlucky in love."

She's relieved when he says, "See you tomorrow in class," and leaves the booth. Maybe she should have let him win, just to make sure he won't punish her when he marks her papers for Canadian Poetry. In the first class, he told the students he was a hard marker. "Tough but fair," he said. "Like Caligula." She had no idea what he meant.

Virgilia is about to put on her boots when two guys stomp in from the creaky porch, their boots clacking over the hardwood floors. After they hang up their jackets, one of them goes to the counter. The other makes a beeline for her booth.

He's short but muscular and is wearing a white long-sleeved top with the words *Surfer Shack* in blue, right over his heart. The guy sits down, sees the ripped upholstery, and lifts himself over the tear. Observant and classy. Then he challenges her to a game of trictrac, correctly assuming that Virgilia speaks French. When she asks him to place *un dollar* on the table, he puts down a fiver.

He's a tough opponent, decisive and fast. Virgilia man-ages to beat him two games in a row. He smokes Gitanes nonstop, and the smoke starts making her dizzy. He says he's from Toulouse, passing through Ottawa to get his passport renewed at the French embassy. He's gruff yet gallant, kind of like Giancarlo Giannini in *A Night Full of Rain*. Much more appealing than Professor Nave, who, she now notices, has left Pigeon Bleu. The two women he came with are still sitting at the bar. The place is full. Someone starts playing a guitar in the corner.

The man across from her rolls the dice again. Virgilia can't tell his precise age, thirties possibly, like Pamela and the professor, somewhere between her and her parents. He orders shots, tries to get her to down one. Virgilia takes a sip, and when she exhales, it feels like smoke is pouring out of her nostrils.

He shows her his special dice, says they're of jade, that he picked them up in Taipei. "*Je suis marin,*" he says. Virgilia has to work to ignore his physical presence, the dangerous diamond stud in one earlobe, his tiger eyes, and the deftly moving hands nicked with scars. "Your French is good," he says. "Where are you from?"

"Montréal."

"And your parents? This country is full of immigrants, no?"

"Estonia." He reminds her of a Russian sailor she once met in Tallinn when she was sixteen, but she doesn't tell him that. She tries to keep her eyes on his and avoid conversation, like she always does with her marks.

"My parents are from Morocco," he says, then asks if they could play with his dice. The two green cubes are beautiful to hold, smaller than the plastic versions she usually plays with, just as heavy if not heavier. When it's his turn to toss them, he snaps his wrist before rolling the dice, actually more like dropping them at an angle, very controlled. He throws an inordinate sequence of double-sixes.

After several games, he's hit her for all her winnings. "I have to go," she says. It's her rule to leave as soon as she's on a losing streak.

"I'll be back tomorrow night. Meet me here?"


WEDNESDAY MORNING, in her apartment on Somerset, she stands in her cubbyhole of a kitchen waiting for the water to boil for coffee. On the fridge door, a rainbow magnet holds her list of 1977 New Year's resolutions. Study harder, exercise every day, stop going to Pigeon Bleu. Two out of three violated and it's only three weeks into January. She takes her mug of coffee and sits at the table by the windows. Oh, those windows! The six-foot panels of curved glass look out at the street. They're the main reason she rented the apartment back in September. The windows plus the rent of eighty bucks per month. Only after she moved into the house, a former mansion split into small apartments rented out to students, did she realize that the place has no closet space and just two electrical outlets. At night, when she's home, people passing by on Somerset can see what she's doing. "It's like living in a fishbowl," her mother pointed out.

She opens her notebook and reaches for the stack of books she's supposed to read for Professor Nave's class, including his debut collection, published by a press in Ottawa four years ago. Leafing through the book, Virgilia deduces that, after the poet's wife left him, he took up with various lovers, all with sad outcomes. The nature poems feel pastoral and Wordsworthy, most having to do with a small town nestled "safe" in his Maritime province. His allusion to "safe" turns her off considering that wasn't how she felt when she was playing backgammon with him last night. If he's good looking, it's in a bland way, *kanadisch*, her mother would say. Virgilia could still drop the class and take another one, but she really wants to learn about contemporary Canadian poetry, and Professor Nave's course is the only one available in the winter semester.

Recently, she's been reading Montréal poets like Irving Layton and Leonard Cohen. In their poetry, Virgilia recognizes her home city and her feelings of anguish and betrayal in the few relationships (maybe three) she's had so far. While they tend to objectify women, at least their writing isn't obscure or pretentious. You could read a Layton poem once and get what he's saying. But the decision to take a contemporary Canadian poetry class was clinched when she went to a reading last fall.

In a large darkened room at the University of Ottawa, the poet stood in a single spotlight while the packed audience of students and others sat on the floor or leaned against the back wall. Dorothy Livesay was old—over sixty, she admitted—but her words sizzled. She was so unlike the poets and professors Virgilia had previously encountered. Livesay was famous but not arrogant, gentle but not submissive, smart but not confusing or show-offy, compassionate but not corny. When Livesay read "The Unquiet Bed," the last stanza ripped into Virgilia's heart: *The woman I am / is not what you see / move over love / make room for me.*

After the reading, she'd gone back to her apartment and written a poem. The next day, another two, and a week later, four more. Now, her poetry fills two notebooks, which she hides under her bed in case friends drop by to visit.

When she leaves the apartment for class, the frigid air emboldens her to take the shortcut over the canal again. Virgilia takes it in leaps, a good dozen, flinging herself across as quickly as possible, hearing creak-crack after every step. The sensations would make for a poem—the airborne hovering, the exhilaration of landing, and the crunchiness of fear colliding with the exuberance she feels.

Virgilia arrives to class fired up but still doesn't dare say a word. Although, at some point, she'll have to say something. Professor Nave said class participation counts for a third of the mark. Virgilia needs to get really high marks, at least B-pluses, to bump up her average in this final year.

She sits at the back, watching Professor Nave perform. He's wearing the same checked shirt as last night but with a black sweater over it, his hair mussed as if he just left his bed.

Perched on the desk, his boots drip melted snow onto the tiled floor. A puddle forms as he speaks. "Canadian poetry is still in its infancy," he says. "You'll be doing groundbreaking work." Then he passes around a bunch of chapbooks and tells the students to pick one and write a review, due next week. "Five pages, double spaced, no typos, your name and student number on the upper right-hand side of the first page." Then he starts his lecture and Virgilia takes notes.

"You, back there…Virge, anything to add?" Professor Nave is staring at her. The student next to Virgilia murmurs, "He wants to know about our favourite Canadian poets."

"Dorothy Livesay?"

"Ah, the feminist poet! Good for you."

After class, Virgilia thanks the student who bailed her out. She says her name's Marie and that she wants to be a journalist. As they leave the arts building, Marie says, "Let's go infiltrate a bastion of the patriarchy!" She means a tavern down in the market. Virgilia agrees, figuring she'll still have time to make it to Pigeon Bleu by eight.

They share a pitcher of draft and take turns picking songs on the jukebox. By the time Virgilia walks all the way up to Pigeon Bleu, she's freezing. The wind seems to blow across the canal with vicious intent. Her mouth feels cottony after the draft beer. Pamela greets her with a wave from behind the dark wood counter. All the booths are taken and most of the little round tables too. Ben serves platefuls of nachos and sandwiches to the tables. Virgilia hangs her coat on a hook as she looks around. In a far corner, three men are sitting at a table with a backgammon game already laid out. Surferman calls her over.

He gets up and kisses her cheeks, finds a chair and drags it to the table. "*Alors, un peu de trictrac ma belle?*" He slaps a ten-dollar bill on the table.

She shakes her head. Not so fast, buddy. She's already folded the rest of her money into the pocket of her jeans. A total of eight dollars, which she plans to double, if not triple, so she can go grocery shopping. "Two dollars a game. That's my limit."

He sets up the board and places the jade dice on the table. "Go ahead." One of the men snickers. "Don't pay attention to him. Guys, get lost." The two men slide their chairs back and walk to the counter. Pamela brings a bowl of steaming milk and two biscotti, sets them by the board. She eyes Surferman. "Another tequila?" Virgilia senses the caution in her movements, as if Pamela is telling her to be careful.

After Virgilia warms her hands on the bowl, she picks up the dice and makes her moves, concentrating on the board. Surferman wins the first game, loses the second, and then wins three more consecutive games. Ben comes over. "Let's see those dice?" He looks at them through his thick Buddy Holly glasses. His hair is almost as long as Pamela's, who once told Virgilia that he refuses to cut off his ponytail until he can go back home to Charleston. He's a draft dodger with the biggest heart in Ottawa, or so Pamela says.

Surferman doesn't say anything. He looks a little danger-ous, like his arms are flexing for a fight. He reaches for the dice in Ben's hands, puts them in his pocket, gets up, and goes to the bathroom.

Ben says, "Hey, I don't know about this guy."

Virgilia nods, pays Pamela for the milk and biscuits. She

puts on her coat and heads for the door. Surferman intercepts her. "Why are you running off?"

"I've got to study."

He follows her out to the patio. "I'll accompany you home. It's late. You shouldn't be out alone."

"Ottawa's safe," she tells him, knowing that's not quite true.

He shrugs. "My passport's supposed to be ready on Friday. I'll be leaving soon. Meet me here tomorrow night?"

Surferman is still standing outside, on the patio, when she glances back before turning right onto Colonel By Drive.

HER PARENTS have no idea about the backgammon, though after two and a half years in Ottawa, they understand she's up to things they can't fathom. They're open-minded compared to her friends' parents. Over Christmas, her mother encouraged Virgilia to take the pill if she ever falls in love, but she knows her parents feel she's young and naive for her nineteen years. At her age, they were fleeing through Europe, scrounging for food and dodging bombs. She also knows that her mother's weekly calls are intended to talk sense into her daughter, to remind her of the great privilege and responsibilities of being a full-time student. "For every hour of lectures, you need to study and read for at least four hours!" The other imperative, according to her mother, is following in her footsteps. "You're the second generation of women in our family to attend university. You can't squander your time there!"

Thursday evening, Virgilia sits staring out her room's bay window. She writes a few lines about Surferman and trictrac, the word evoking the sounds of backgammon pieces moving during a game. She's attracted to him, she concludes, partly because he's dangerous but mostly because he's unslottable, a bit like her. He doesn't figure in the category of any other person she's encountered in Ottawa. Not a student from small-town Ontario or a professor. Not a civil servant. Not a draft dodger. Not Canadian, not even totally French. She wonders whether his parents are from Casablanca, like the movie, and why she doesn't even know his real name. She tries to envisage what he was like as a kid, and soon she's invented his history, his siblings, imagines him climbing ropes on a ship like a pirate and playing trictrac in the dark alleys of a mysterious port city.

She begins a poem, "Surferman," but the word *unslottable* is not conducive to poetry. She thinks *unstoppable*, which is how she'd like to be in life. Determined, clear in her strivings. But toward what goal? Thinking back to her games with him, how he seemed to win more than statistically likely, Virgilia gets angry at herself for falling for his politesse and the obvious "let's use my dice" ploy. He's not interested in her as a person. She's just his mark. Like all the civil servants who are just her marks.

She tries writing a few more lines. It's dark outside, but snow is falling through the halo of lights on the street. When she looks up again, she sees a bulky figure in a jacket staring into her windows, his dark hair covered in snow. In the foreground, her undulating reflection is mirrored in the windows. How long has he been out there? She reaches for the lamp on her table, turns off the light.

On Friday, it snows all day. Virgilia picks up some groceries on Elgin Street and then sits at her table, working on the review for Professor Nave's class. The assignment has a real-life quality, like something you'd actually have to do at a magazine or newspaper. She spends all morning rereading *The Chemistry of Instruments* by Jane Jordan, taking notes and marking the pages she likes, from the opening poem, "Ottawa," to the last one, on page forty-eight, "Brass Notes," each stanza speaking truths she'd rarely encountered in poetry. Like Dorothy Livesay's words but even more intense.

As in, *Gestures are the poem / you write / to tell me / the world is fragile*. It feels like the poet is addressing her in very precise terms, because the poems Virgilia scribbles in her notebooks expose her own fragility. The hardest part of crafting the review is to remain soberly unbiased. That's what Marie said good journalism is all about—impartial, serious, and smart, the arguments building indisputably. The second hardest part is coming up with an opening line. Virgilia paces her apartment until, at last, she's ready to write the final version. "With a pen in one hand and a magnifying glass in the other, Jane Jordan...." She types the five pages, and when she's finally done, it's dark outside again.

Virgilia puts on her long denim skirt and a sweater, takes her coat, and picks up her dice from the bookshelf by the door.

The snow is deep on the footpath along Queen Elizabeth Drive. There's a crew working on the canal. A few cross-country skiers swish past. A man walks a lab that rolls around in the powdery snow. Friday night and Ottawa feels like a village. What did Jane Jordan say about the city? *Living in a city of politics / I sit on a bench & watch helplessly / the sins of omission.*

Crossing Pretoria Bridge over the canal, she sees Pigeon Bleu in all its lit-up glory. A beacon. Outside, a couple of guys are sharing a joint. The moonglow emblazons the patio's snow with a mysterious blue light.

When Virgilia enters the bar, she can barely move through the crowds, has to edge over to the coat rack. All the hooks are taken, so she keeps her coat on. Ben's southern voice booms from across the bar. Virgilia hardly recognizes him. His hair's cut short, not a crewcut but the ponytail's gone. Someone has tacked a handmade sign on the dartboard: *Freedom Friday January 21, 1977* encircled with a red heart.

Pamela waves her over to the counter and yells over the noise. "First drink's on the house!"

"What's going on?" Virgilia thinks that maybe Pamela and Ben have announced their engagement. They love each other, that she knows, but they don't seem like the marrying type.

"Haven't you heard? Jimmy Carter got inaugurated yesterday. Today he announced the pardons! Draft dodgers can go back home without facing arrest."

Pamela hands her a bowl of hot milk, takes a bottle of Kahlua, and pours a shot into the creamy liquid. "You don't drink, but you'll like this."

It's standing-room-only and there's not a single civil servant in sight.

"I don't think you'll get any games in today," Pamela says.

Surferman is standing by a booth. Virgilia takes a few sips of the spiked milk. Then she smells the Gitanes and knows he's right beside her. "How about some trictrac?" he asks.

"*Non, merci.*"

"Just one game. And you'll never see me again."

"Where? It's too crowded." She can see that he likes her resistance.

"Outside on the terrace."

"It's too cold." But she follows him outside.

Surferman sweeps the snow off a table and two chairs, sets up the board, and produces his jade dice from a jacket pocket. They shine in the moonlight, as glittery as the snow all around them.

Virgilia takes out her dice from the pocket of her denim skirt. "Tonight we'll use mine." She places two dollars on the table.

"*Non, pas d'argent.*" He rubs his hands together and blows on them. "I win, I walk you home." He lights a smoke and the flare from his match reflects off the diamond stud in his earlobe.

Surferman senses her reluctance and digs out a coin from his pocket. "My lucky franc. First coin I ever won in trictrac. Either way, you get to keep it."

Virgilia pockets her money and lets him place the franc in her palm. The coin feels so warm in her hand. She looks straight into Surferman's tiger eyes and nods.

# BRAVER THAN ANYONE

THE EYES OF THE TAXI DRIVER regard me in the mirror. "Why are you going out in this storm?" The sky is dark in the downpour even though it's the summer solstice and well before sunset. I mention a poetry reading and his thick eyebrows rise. He turns off the radio, inhales deeply, and begins to recite a poem in Farsi. I don't understand him but I discern a music in his cadence. From previous rides with this company, I know that the founders are Iranian. Many of their drivers are former air force pilots who fought in the Iran-Iraq War, an eight-year conflict that ended in 1988. Already twenty years ago, I realize. Since then, I've listened to the drivers lament the suffering in their country whenever I've splurged on a taxi ride through the streets of Montréal. But until now, I'd never heard any of them speak in verse.

As the cab snakes uphill into Westmount, the trees and houses become larger. On a narrow street, we pass into a tunnel of leafy branches. The metallic staccato of rainfall on the car ceases. In front of the consular residence, the driver switches off the windshield wipers and shuts off the motor. The residence is an ordinary stone mansion, no traces of the national emblems—the black-red-yellow flag or the eagle flexing its wings that were embossed on the invitation mailed to me a few weeks ago. The pre-printed text on the manila card announced that the *Generalkonsul der Bundesrepublik Deutschland* [and his wife] *have the honour of inviting.........* *to a reading by Professor Gustav Hasenbach (Ottawa) from the works by Walter Bauer and from his own works on Friday, 20 June 2008 at 18:30.* My surprise at receiving the invitation in the first place catapulted into shock when I noticed that the handwritten script on the dotted line, inviting me and a guest, matched my mother's emphatic cursive.

A rusted Volkswagen pulls up in front of the taxi. A man with white hair emerges and heaves a briefcase up the stairs to the residence. The door opens and he disappears inside.

The driver pleads, "One more poem, Miss, just one."

The sounds of the words to the patter of rain are beautiful and familiar. The mansion is not. I'm tempted to stay inside the dark and humid cab, but in the end I pay my fare and run up the stairs through the rain.

> *I saw you in the hospitals*
> *and in the line*
> *of political prisoners...*
> *Muse, wherever you*
> *might go*
> *I go.*
> *I follow your radiant trail*
> *across the long night...*
>
> –from "Muse" by Roberto Bolaño

I accept a glass of champagne and gaze out of the living room window onto sodden treetops. Aside from one acquaintance—a Québécois man with wavy hair who owns a bookstore and once urged me to read Stefan Zweig—I don't recognize anyone in the animated clusters around me. I look down and realize we're all standing on a blood-red Persian carpet.

Not far down the hill, on Sherbrooke and Saint-Catherine Streets, the cafés and terraces are filling in while musicians set up amps and drum kits in basement bars. I could be there, among the crowds. This is the time of year when Montréal resurfaces to celebrate the lingering light of the longest day and the shortest of nights. The ice has long melted, the waterways have opened, festival stages occupy the streets and buskers blossom by the seductive scents of lilacs and jasmine in the back-alleys of Plateau Mont-Royal.

In this city of exiles, when poets gather to listen to other poets, it's a gesture of solidarity. By going to readings, I help keep this marginalized form of art from disappearing. Writing poetry, struggling with words and sounds, space and silence, requires affirmation. I flourish to the words of other writers. I'm still glowing from the sublime recital in the taxicab.

Readings often leave me unhinged. The few listeners in attendance, the shabbiness of the venues, the fragility of the artists, some teetering on the knife's edge of existence. Afterward, walking home in the dark, I'm resurrected by the divinity of poetry but also left wretched by its futility. It's a risk to expose the subconscious to unknown poetry. The German word for poet is *Dichter*, stemming from the adjective *dicht*, which appropriately means compact, dense. But there's also *Dichterling*, or poetaster, a potentially contagious condition. I take another glass of champagne to inoculate myself.

An urgent clapping of hands silences the chatter. I carry my glass into an adjacent room, where rows of chairs are arranged in a semicircle around an armchair. No carpets on the hardwood floor. Soaked shoes squeak into the room. Some paintings hang on the white walls, and a window looks out onto the rain.

The *Generalkonsul*, balding and unusually tanned for June, welcomes us to the reading. "We are honoured to host you in our residence," he says, smiling at the latecomers who squeak into their seats while he speaks. "Tonight we have in our presence a distinguished professor from Ottawa. *Herr Doktor* Hasenbach will be entertaining us with thought-provoking works. I, for one, am looking forward to an evening of reflection, a salve in our hectic times."

During the short speech, the professor sits before us in an armchair, the very same person I saw emerging from the Volkswagen outside, and rummages in his briefcase. He extracts a sheaf of papers, then drinks from a glass of water thoughtfully left for him on the coffee table.

After the introduction, the *Generalkonsul* sits down next to his wife. Two empty chairs over, a lanky man with a scar punctuating his cheek folds his arms across his chest, as if settling in for a nap.

The invitation promised that a professor would be reading the poetry of the late Walter Bauer. Before leaving home, I'd googled the name and discovered that Walter Bauer (1877–1960) was a theologian who wrote that heresy was actually the original manifestation of early Christianity. The search did not yield any citations of Walter Bauer's poetry, but I expect dense, heavy lyrics that will stretch my comprehension of German.

The handwriting on the invitation has compelled me, as if dispatched by my mother on an urgent mission, to come here for language practice.

Professor Hasenbach, with his white hair and pink face, resembles a nervous rabbit. "Good evening," he begins, and I'm pleased to understand his *guten Abend*. "Thank you for your presence."

He coughs, drinks more water, and then removes four books from his briefcase. A painting on the wall above his head portrays a landscape, possibly Algonquin Park, with a lonely red-leaved maple tree.

"The late Walter Bauer was my close friend and colleague," Professor Hasenbach confesses. "A prolific poet and author of an impressive list of books, ninety published works and 600 unpublished poems, Walter Bauer left Germany in the sixties disgusted by the cynicism of the postwar reconstruction."

In Toronto, the professor tells us, Walter Bauer washed dishes to pay his way through grad school at U of T. There's no mention of his theology. It dawns on me that tonight's Walter Bauer is not the same one I researched on the internet. While I'm relieved that my German, so far, seems to be holding up, I had hoped for some deeper illumination.

At this point, Professor Hasenbach digresses into his own life, explaining how he left Germany at a very young age and refused for many decades to speak his mother tongue. Then, as if embarrassed to have inserted his own biography into that of his friend's, he introduces a poem by Walter Bauer. "It was," he says, "written in the 1920s."

He clears his throat and reads the poem. His delivery is dramatic and clear enough, but I have to focus entirely on the words to absorb their meaning. The lines describe how two uniformed thugs beat up a worker for no reason. The violence of the scene, several stanzas long, has all of us leaning forward in our seats except the man with the scar, whose arms remain folded across his chest. For me, the poem is a striking reminder of how the decade preceding the war foreshadowed the eventual horrors.

Having completed reciting the poem, the professor regards us. "Walter Bauer, unlike many writers, did not leave the country." By this, I assume he means that Bauer stayed even after Hitler was elected by the people of Germany and then endured the war there. Unlike other writers who did leave, like Thomas Mann. He moves on to later poems by Bauer, written after his immigration to Toronto. One describes the sun in Canada as different, having no guilt or shame.

The professor can't resist sharing one of his own poems about the Canadian North. It features a lonely tree in a barren landscape to evoke, he notes in his introduction to the poem, how he felt when facing his new adoptive country after being displaced and abandoned. He looks up at us and confesses, "We did not always see eye to eye, Walter Bauer and I." There's a shocking candour in his admission, and I notice the *Generalkonsul* crossing his leg then uncrossing it quickly, as if nervous, or at least impatient, about what's coming next. "I personally believe the sun shining here is the same one you see in Germany."

A woman next to me requests a specific poem by Walter Bauer. The professor rifles through his briefcase. There's coughing and shuffling of feet as he searches the various compartments. Saving him further embarrassment, the *Generalkonsul* announces an intermission.

We all rise, liberated from our hard chairs. Double doors open to a garden. The rain has stopped, so I head toward a chestnut tree laden with conical blossoms still wet from the rains and shimmering white against the dusky sky. Smokers congregate around an ashtray. A few guests approach me, including two elderly women, widows perhaps, whose demeanours and clothing evoke a European formality. From their excited remarks, it appears that they are familiar with Walter Bauer. One even knew him personally.

"Such an exceptional poet," she says.

Not to be outdone, the other responds, "He's been tragically overlooked, don't you find?"

I can't bring myself to admit that, before tonight, I'd never heard of Walter Bauer.

The ladies move on to other guests, and left alone, I look around for my Québécois acquaintance. But he seems to have remained inside. Or perhaps he's taken advantage of the intermission to escape the sequestered event. I want to report to him that, following his urging, I did indeed read a Stefan Zweig novella, and that I appreciated its feverish quality. Zweig left Austria in the thirties and moved to England, New York, and then Brazil, where he and his wife died, in 1942, in an apparent double suicide. I want to ask my acquaintance, "Why did you want me to read Zweig? Was it his works or his biography? Do you know that my mother also immigrated to Brazil? Do you know what I know about suicide?"


THERE'S A CLAPPING of hands. Everyone hurries back into the residence to occupy the exact same chairs in the semicircle.

With relish, Professor Hasenbach announces that he's found the poem requested before the intermission. After reading it, he speaks of the bravery implicit in Walter Bauer's verses. "The poet possessed a courage he demonstrated again and again in his life."

He refers to a letter Walter Bauer wrote to a publisher, in the early 1940s, in defence of a writer banned by the Nazis. "This proves how brave Walter Bauer was," he says with a tremor. Then he proceeds to read the letter. The dense language, the use of honorifics, and the careful selection of words so as not to appear too demanding or insistent all suggest a carefully crafted missive, one not wanting to alienate yet at the same time appealing to the publisher's humanity toward the banned writer. From our twenty-first-century perspective, the letter is much too long, yet I feel for its writer, sitting at his typewriter in an attic somewhere in Stuttgart, drafting and redrafting his agonizing words.

During the rambling text, I recall my one visit to the German consulate, which may account for my name appearing among the invitees to this reading. Inside an office tower with southeast views over the port of Montréal and the widening waters of the Saint-Laurent, I was waiting to have a translation of my mother's death certificate stamped and notarized. A guard stood in a corner, holding a semiautomatic weapon. His watchful silence made me feel guilty, as if I were responsible for my own mother's death, which had caused the officials—and, by extension, him—so much trouble.

As the professor reads, my mother's image appears to me from 1945, well before my existence, in a frantic scene she'd often described to us as children. Fleeing the Russians, she sat jammed in a train car. Just before crossing the Oder River, they heard the unmistakable drone of approaching planes. The train ground to a halt. Screaming passengers grabbed children and bags and ran off into the snowy fields. My mother chose to remain on the train. She witnessed bombs dropping and bodies collapsing. The planes retreated and she waited alone in her car through the dark, cold silence. At dawn, the train slowly jolted back to life and continued toward the British army advancing in the west.

A few nights ago, while grappling with whether to attend this reading, I found some documents my mother had managed to salvage when fleeing. There were papers from her high school, dated 1942, the same school attended years earlier by the wife of Claus von Stauffenberg, the brave woman who gave birth to her last child in prison after her husband was executed for his failed assassination attempt on Hitler.

Looking around, I observe that the dimensions of this room are similar to those where Stauffenberg planted the bomb in a briefcase in July 1944. Hitler and his officers were protected by a thick oak table when the bomb detonated. An explosive planted in this living room would kill us all.

The professor says, "Walter Bauer taught literature at a Canadian university, no easy task for a German expatriate. He loathed the likes of Kafka, preferring more optimistic writers, but was forced to teach him."

This bothers me, Bauer's dismissal of Kafka. I wonder how he felt about Rilke, whose diaries' self-loathing and darkness seem to out-Kafka Kafka himself. My mother often mentioned how Rilke's poems helped her get through the war. But, shortly before her death, she claimed his poetry no longer stirred her in the same way it did decades earlier. I argued with her at the time, though I've come to understand her position. Some writers and their works become markers for a certain phase in our lives. And then we transition, become someone else. My admiration for Neruda when I was twenty has, three decades later, evolved into subdued respect.

The professor welcomes questions. A woman asks, "What was Walter Bauer's position on Canadian identity when this issue was debated during the 1970s?"

"There is no such thing as Canadian identity," the professor replies. "We are all just human beings." This strikes me as sensible enough, until he goes one step further and adds that he left Québec at the time because he couldn't stand all the protesters shouting *Québec pour les québécois*. "Too nationalistic," he says.

Silence. Then the *Generalkonsul* rises to thank the professor and presents him with an envelope to sporadic applause.

*Poetry slips into dreams*
*like a diver in a lake.*
*Poetry, braver than anyone,*
*slips in and sinks...*
–from "Resurrection" by Roberto Bolaño

I follow the stampede to the dining room and take some cucumber sandwiches. The two ladies I met during intermission fill their plates with every manner of delicacy. Their enthusiasm for the refreshments brings to mind people I've observed at book launches who seem to appreciate the wine and cheese more than the books themselves. Looking at the table spread, I regret not bringing a poet friend in need of nourishment (I can think of many!) to accompany me tonight. But how many of the Montréal poets I know understand German? Interrupting my thoughts, Professor Hasenbach skitters into the dining room to promote his new book. His hair in a wild white flurry, he works the room for half an hour and then packs Bauer's books back into his bag, ready to return to Ottawa.

The man with the scar on his cheek introduces himself. "I overheard you speaking German earlier," he says. "I'm curious about your dialect."

"I learned German from my mother. She was born in Estonia"

"Well, I was born in Germany during the war. I can't understand why the professor had to bring up guilt and shame!"

"My father-in-law survived Mauthausen and moved to Argentina after the war. He speaks of his time in the concentration camp," I say. "And, although his German is good, he prefers to speak with me in Spanish. It's his way of resisting."

"My father fought for the *Wehrmacht* in France and Russia. He came home in 1945 and never spoke of it once."

"He should have."

The man's face reddens except for the scar, a cruel comma demarking his cheek.

Some expressive silences work as resistant affirmations within works of beauty. Others, like this one, are haunted by denial. Later, when analyzing what I could have possibly said to change his mind, I will invoke Kafka's words: *I had to restrain myself from putting my arm around his shoulders and kissing him on the eyes as a reward for having absolutely no use for me.*

The *Generalkonsul* sidles up, takes my arm in a placating

manner, and tells me he was once posted in Estonia, shortly after the country's independence. He leads me to the door and, handing me a pen, asks that I sign the guestbook. I scan the German written by others, short phrases like *Danke schön* and *gute Nacht*. I write *Danke Nacht* and depart into the dark.

Shifting clouds reveal a radiant trail of stars over the distant river. I walk downhill, past the mansions, toward the beckoning razzle-dazzle of Montréal on a Friday night, the streetlights on this longest day of the year just beginning to glow. I see them form the grid of streets both linear and curvy, see the bridge down below alight with the red tail lights of cars. All to the sounds of rainwater dripping from the trees. And, between each drop, silence.

# LILY METTERLING & HER
# MACHO IDIOTS

ARRIVING EARLY, I select a table by the window and fold my coat on the banquette. I slide into the sunlight, open my knapsack, and stack Lily Metterling's two novels on the table so she'll be able to identify me, a strategy I learned in Buenos Aires from reviewers of my works. Authors, especially splashy ones with publicists, can spot their beloved books a city block away.

The server approaches, a graceful apparition with long black hair, possibly Argentine like me, but I don't go there. I ask for a glass of water pending Lily's arrival. "Two beverages only, Saskia," the editor of *Ragged* specified when she assigned me the tasks of interviewing Lily Metterling and reviewing her latest book. This was after our brouhaha over my last expense claim involving a wine-soaked author interview.

It's a frigid Montréal day but clear, the only clouds created by buildings spewing steam. When I first witnessed this phenomenon, on a bitter Christmas Day a few weeks ago, I feared the buildings were on fire. To warm up, I chew on ice cubes, one of several tricks I've acquired to counter the freezing weather here. Decreasing body temperature makes the ambience feel less cold.

Last night, I finished reading Lily's latest novel, *Men with Weird Names*, and as I wait, I try to imagine how it would be translated into French (*Les hommes aux noms bizarres?*) and Spanish (*Hombres con nombres extraños?*). The book is a catalogue of encounters—sexual, intellectual—that the protagonist, an exiled poet, has with men in far-flung corners of the globe.

The title of each chapter is the man's name, some of them not that weird. Foreign, maybe, and Lily's labelling of them in this manner only confirms her provincialism. The last chapter, "Boyo," is about motherhood and the baby boy the protagonist has with one of the men. The mystery of the father's identity remains unresolved, and the reader, if interested enough, is obliged to flip back through the chapters to decipher the enigmatic ending.

Instead of doing that, I open my laptop and several emails pop up. There's good news from my publisher in Buenos Aires (translation rights acquired in London) followed by a new diatribe from my ex. He's been drinking; I can tell by his wild swings from the accusatory ("how dare you steal from people's lives for the purposes of your shitty novel") to the meek ("please come back, Saskia, I need you"). I delete his email, aware that, tomorrow, another one will arrive to contaminate my inbox.

Writers don't have a lock on trickery. That's one thing I learned from my ex. When I met him, in a Palermo bar not far from where Borges once lived, Jorge told me that he was a guitarist in a reputable ensemble. I fell for him, his name (just like Borges!), and his wild head of curls, and before I knew it, he was installing his toothbrush in my bathroom and a high-end sound system in my living room.

A year or so later, I spotted Jorge busking to tourists in a plaza in San Telmo, which led to the discovery that our comfortable existence had been a fraudulent fabrication enabled by funding from his wealthy (but, I thought, estranged) family. These were the oligarchs I'd subjected to "truth-fictionalizing" in my novel. They're proprietors of a tobacco plantation in the north, a bucolic feudal estate stretching over an Andean plain. But *tobacco*—what decent writer could resist the implicit decadence in that deathly metaphor? After my splashy launch at the former cinema converted into a bookstore, the parents flew down to Buenos Aires for damage control. The tabloids trumpeted allegations ("Saskia Martinez accused of libel by her in-laws!") as if it were a crime, rather than the essence of literature, to make art out of life. My publicist, cowed by oligarchic threats, quit on the spot.

So as not to poison my mind with ex-related venom, I browse for further news on the feud between Leo Pluma and Jordi Goya, which has been unfolding lately in cliff-hanging episodes as catty as the worst Argentine telenovela. In English-language publications, their feud is being compared to the Julian Barnes/Martin Amis debacle, Salman Rushdie's outburst about John Updike, and the long-ago Norman Mailer attack on Gore Vidal. But, in Spanish venues, the writers' differences are being plotted along "Europe versus Latin America" lines, in language that resembles World Cup postgame diatribes.

What captivates me about the feud, beyond its voyeuristic quality, has more to do with a literary gathering I attended last spring. On a rainy Friday evening not long after my arrival in Montréal, I attended a talk between these two writers in the back of a Spanish-language bookstore.

In his distinctly Mexican Spanish, the owner of the bookstore introduced the writers with the usual descriptions of books published and prizes garnered. To his left, the older Leo Pluma sat hunched over pages of notes. He was a swarthy man with black-rimmed glasses, his demeanour sad but not hostile. Next to him, Jordi Goya leaned comfortably against the back of his chair, a bright-orange scarf folded in half and looped around his neck. Jordi looked out at us from beneath frenzied curls, seeking eye contact and occasionally smiling at the audience. All thirteen of us occupied the folding chairs with only two vacant seats in the front. Most were displaced Latinos, and I recognized many of them. If Montréal's literary world is a beehive, then the subset of Spanish-speaking writers is just a little honeycomb. Miniscule.

Billed as a discussion on "the meaning of place in fictional narrative," the event was part of a trilingual festival in this modest city I temporarily call home. "Modest" may be a disputed characterization of Montréal, but it's meant as a compliment, in the sense of "restrained" or "unpretentious," relative to greater Buenos Aires, which is neither modestly sized, with 13 million-plus inhabitants, nor lacking brashness. I was at the festival thanks to *Ragged*, the online magazine that had secured my pass in exchange for a few articles about the authors featured.

The moderator opened the discussion rather unimaginatively. "What is the role of geography in your novels?"

Leo Pluma began with an anecdote about walking through Central Park in a snowstorm while suffering nostalgia for his birth city of Madrid, and how his commotion of feelings inspired his latest novel. I hadn't read the two writers' recent works and wasn't sure whether I'd have the time to read (or the money to buy) their books. But I enjoyed listening to the cadence of the Spanish and Leo's low-key delivery as he talked about how much easier it is to write of his birthplace when he's elsewhere.

When it was Jordi's turn, he invoked an insane asylum in Argentina and how that place became a metaphor in one of his novels. He talked about a "geography of the interior," which he claimed was more interesting than physical landscapes. "I'm not big on description," he said, with a disparaging glance at Leo, "or nostalgia."

Before he could elaborate, there was an interruption as a tall latecomer walked up the aisle, blond hair swinging down her back. She had to cross in front of the writers to get to one of the empty chairs. Although she presumably knew nothing of me, I immediately recognized Lily Metterling, a local author who'd made a splash with her first novel, *I Like It Slow*, translated into thirteen languages including French (*Tranquillement, mon amour*) and Spanish (*Más despacio, querido*).

Lily took her seat, arching her back to shrug a damp trench coat off her shoulders. I was close enough to smell the citrusy trace of her perfume and see Jordi's eyes widen. Beside him, Leo Pluma smoothed back his dyed hair and tried to sit a little straighter. Meanwhile, Lily rummaged in her purse for a pen and pad, the rings on her fingers catching the bookstore's overhead lights.

For the remaining hour or so, the two writers promoted their novels without any swipes or hogging of the audience's attention. Looking back, I do recall Leo trying to trump Jordi's natural charm with some flattering commentary about the Canadian literary scene, mentioning that he'd reviewed and/ or interviewed some Famous Writers, mangling their names, regrettably, with his Spanish pronunciation. Discreetly, both men kept checking Lily Metterling's reactions to their erudite utterances.

When the talk ended, I hung around the shelves, furtively browsing the bookstore as I listened to Diego glower in the background about "Argentines really needing all those psychotherapists."

THE SERVER is vigorously wiping off the tables in the café, empty but for me and a couple leaning against the counter, friends of the server keeping her company on this very quiet Tuesday morning. She's edging toward my table. Lily's late. What can I do except contemplate ordering a coffee pending her arrival?

Finally, having reached the table next to mine, the server asks, "Would you like anything else?" Her tone is friendly, I'm relieved to note.

"I'll wait until my companion gets here, thanks. But I could handle some more ice cubes."

She nods, glancing at the books on my table. "My friends were wondering...are you Lily Metterling?"

Hell no, I almost chortle. "She's coming any minute now."

"It's just that we love her books. They're so...Montréal."

Really? I ponder this as the server hurries back to inform her friends. Is it that Lily Metterling's globe-trotting sexual encounters ultimately transcend place and speak to twenty-somethings in their language?

Outside the sunny window, the Montréal streets are dead this frigid January morning. It's moments like this when, forgetting its craziness and dangers, I miss my home city, how its nonstop soundtrack matches my mother tongue. Language is the only element of my history that still feels completely grounded.

I go back to my laptop and find Leo Pluma's recent salvo, a *New York Times* essay in which he states, "There has been no memorable Argentine writer since Borges." Jordi Goya responds with a tweet dismissing the "geriatric posturing of frustrated Europeans."

I resolve to get Lily Metterling's take on the feud and scan my list of questions to figure out at which point I should refer back to the literary event in May. I don't want to engage in a sexist *cherchez la blonde* exercise. I just want to know what she makes of their battle.

A stinging mass of cold air precedes Lily's arrival. She takes the chair across from me and unfurls a delicate scarf of grey wool, sunlight glistening off her earrings. Two braids crown her head.

The server hurries to our table. Lily orders a bowl of *chocolat chaud* and slithers out of her coat. I ask for an Americano, milk on the side. My banquette is lower than her chair, giving her a height advantage.

"So you're..." She looks down at her phone. "Saskia? An unusual name, Rembrandt's wife's, am I right?"

I nod, relieved she used the word *unusual* rather than *weird*. "Is Metterling a German name?"

"Huguenot. From Eastern Prussia, now Poland."

"But you were born here," I say, an assertion to prove I'm familiar with her bio. I also read that Lily Metterling was, like me, orphaned at a young age, and that she studied philosophy in Mexico City (hence her Frida Kahlo look) before writing her first novel. I decide to skip all that. "I just finished reading your new—"

"How did you like it?"

"Intriguing." Her laser-like gaze disconcerts, like an approaching car with its high beams on. I long for sunglasses but lurch forward, asking about the novel's structure, her decisions to write in present tense and play with geography so that every encounter with the man in question occurs in a different location, the landscape often mirroring the psyche of the narrator.

Lily describes how the book took shape as she travelled on tours for her first novel, finding herself at odd little festivals or literary gatherings in an obscure corner of Romania, flying on to Sicily, Slovenia, and Toulouse. "And that's only Europe. I also travelled to Taiwan and Calcutta, Bahrain and Cairo."

The server brings her bowl of hot chocolate and my doll-sized cup of coffee. Blushing, she tells Lily that she and "my friends over there are big fans."

Lily is pleased. Her pale cheeks don't redden; she takes the compliment in stride. But she glances from the server to me. I feel compelled to say, "It seems your work really resonates."

"Where are you from?" Lily asks the server.

"Chile."

"Like Saskia here."

"No, I'm Argentine."

The server regards me with obvious disapproval. Argentines tend to get a bad rap in Latin America, especially the ones from Buenos Aires. Arrogant, we're often called, high maintenance and twitchy. I go for my biggest smile, but the server's sashaying back to her friends at the counter.

"Where was I?" Lily asks.

"Travelling."

"Right. So I extended those experiences to the imaginary, creating invented landscapes, cities, and towns, and placing the character there. I see it as topographical rather than geographic."

She's attempting to prevent me from asking too many questions. I've heard that local reviewers make her nervous. Apparently, she's fine at book fairs in Frankfurt and Guadalajara, but here, she has to contend with the disconcerting inversion of her worldwide acclaim and everyone else's local obscurity. *Notoriety,* I'd love to tell her, *is a short-lived condition with painful symptoms.*

As Lily's winding down from a description of riding a camel on the Jordanian desert alongside a "real nomad" and her profound thirst "to discover nonbelonging," I take the plunge.

"So the meaning of place in your narratives extends to the metaphorical. Not unlike the Latin American tradition of using words to reflect the power of the landscape. I'm thinking for example of Jordi Goya, the Argentine who writes of the megacity as an insane asylum."

Her eyes narrow as if she's willing herself to be shrewd.

"You've read Goya?" I ask.

Lily nods. "Oh yes. I've read his books and I've read *him.*"

At this point, Lily masterfully recounts the May event I attended, catapulting it into a full-blown lecture with hundreds of participants, a "really engaging discussion of metaphysical realities in metafictions." Leo Pluma and Jordi Goya, she says, "were absolutely fascinating despite their opposing views on issues such as how to avoid the chauvinism of writing place in deconstructed narratives." At the end of the event, as she was gathering her things with "the full intention of going home to write, that's how stoked I was," Leo Pluma approached her, claiming, she says, "to have recognized me even though I was sitting at the back of the hall." He invited Lily to join him and Jordi for dinner. Off they went to a cozy bistro with fantastic wines, "three writers in search of common ground."

Lily tilts the bowl to finish her drink. When she continues speaking, two streaks of chocolate parenthesize her nose, momentarily endearing her to me. She describes the meal, who ordered what and the two bottles of wine consumed, "mainly by Leo Pluma. But who am I to criticize? He knows everyone!" At some later point, "before dessert, I think," each of the men left the table to use the toilet. In his absence, the other invited Lily to his hotel room. "They were staying at the same hotel in adjacent rooms, Leo Pluma in 575 and Jordi Goya in 576. After our crèmes brulées with espressos, we said goodbye outside the restaurant. They shared a taxi back to the hotel, each of them expecting me to show up at his hotel room later."

She rubs her nose, smearing a streak of chocolate onto her cheek. I wait.

"If you knew them, or had seen them, I think you'd guess who I might have picked."

Jordi Goya with his striking orange scarf and curly locks,

no doubt. But, switching points of view, I wonder what made the two men fall for Lily Metterling. The unplucked (albeit fair) eyebrows? Her blue-eyed laser gaze? Her unabashed (read: sexual) confidence?

"I couldn't alienate the other," she says, "and risk him seeing me sneaking in or out of his neighbour's room."

And now the two writers are going after each other like duellers in a nineteenth-century novel, their achievements negated by flying gauntlets and misfired pistols. I decide to ask her straight. "What do you make of their feud?"

"Depressingly puerile."

"Do you suppose it's because each thinks the other spent that night in May with you?"

Lily shrugs. "Macho idiots." She laughs. "Maybe that'll be the title of my next book."

"Do you think Leo Pluma will review your novel?"

"My publisher sent him a review copy. I guess, if Leo goes negative, Jordi will defend me."

"And, if he's positive, Jordi will disagree."

"That's where you come in, Saskia."

Lily presses me to write a review not for local readers of *Ragged* curious about the plot of her latest book and seeking vainly for nostalgic references to Montréal's landmarks but for "an international audience" so she can post a link to it on her website. She wants me to compare her (favourably, of course) to writers both established (Leo Pluma) and emerging (Jordi Goya), preempting either from taking a negative position on her book. "You've got the Hispanic background and name recognition. I mean, it'll make sense for you to allude to the two of them. My strategy is to get them to agree on my book and bring an end to their silly feud." And the coup de grâce, "Saskia, it'll redeem what's left of your reputation!"

I remember a trickster I met in Palermo last year, at a dingy bar, just after things fell apart with my ex. Despite the crowded darkness, the trickster had sensed my vulnerability as an easy mark based on the headlines ("Novelist Saskia Martinez haunted by allegations of truth-fictionalizing" alongside my ghostly photo in sunglasses and a trench coat as I escaped into a taxi.) With an earnest audacity similar to Lily's, the fellow, curly haired and twitchy, offered me fifty pesos if I agreed to complicity in a ruse. We'd saunter into a local book antiquarian like two lovers seeking browse-worthy shelving. He (the trickster) would steal a signed first edition of Borges's seminal *Ficciones*. While I created a diversion, faking the loss of a fat wallet full of cash, he'd slip out of the store unnoticed, the book in his knapsack, leaving me to face the owner's pistol, Rottweiler, and my conscience. This encounter with the trickster was the last straw, propelling me to leave my country for good (at least until my visa expires).

A reviewer interviewing an author is accustomed to being the target of some manipulation. But Lily's plan brought "controlling the narrative" to new heights. I listen, showing little reaction, until she adds, "At least I'm sure of one thing: I'm true to my own heart. Don't you think?"

"You've got some chocolate on your face" is all I reply, handing her a napkin. Later, I'll regret my lack of expressed outrage since silence has enabled so many evils.

I WIND UP writing a genuine review of *Men with Weird Names*. It takes many drafts to neutralize the tone. I avoid

(Plumian) ad hominem attacks and try not to fall into the "reviewmanship" trap whereby the reviewer tries to come off as smarter than her subject. I praise what I like (the invented settings, the immediacy of the prose) and play down the faults (the premise, the unflinching arrogance of the first-person narrator, the sentimental take on motherhood) except for one: the complete absence of (Goyaesque) nonbinary possibility, a failing that readers should be mindful of before swooning over Lily Metterling's prose.

The weeks go by slowly as I struggle through the brutal conditions of my first Montréal winter. I land a few reading gigs at the university thanks to a Latina professor and make some progress on my new novel. Not long after accepting and paying me for my piece, the editor of *Ragged* sends me an email claiming that "limited resources," etc., etc., preclude her from commissioning further work from me.

I struggle with the urge to post some scathing remark on social media about Lily Metterling, who I assume is responsible for my dismissal. She hasn't responded to my review, "Writers with Weird Egos," a title that seemed clever at the time but verges on that Argentine arrogance I'm still trying hard to shed.

At least the royalties from my novels seem to be on the upswing thanks to the notoriety back home. As for my interview, posted alongside the review, a mostly truthful reportage that took me hours to polish up, the editor of *Ragged* begrudgingly thanked me "for all the traction." I'm especially proud of the ending, in which I deliver, for the readers' sheer entertainment, this imaginary conversation over breakfast, setting the stage for the subsequent verbal boxing match:

| Leo: | Great dinner last night! That Lily Schmetterling, what a delight! |
|---|---|
| Jordi: | Metterling. Get her name right, old man. [I'd written *viejo* for the sake of verisimilitude, but alas, the editors insisted on English throughout.] |
| Leo: | You wouldn't happen to have any aspirin? My head...the cheap wine... |
| Jordi: | No. Actually, she disappointed, given all the acclaim. Where's the intellectual? The cleverness? And, above all, the passion? |
| Leo: | I think we must have overwhelmed her. You should be more restrained. |
| Jordi: | How so? |
| Leo: | Charm is earned, my friend [*amigo*, I'd written]. Not doled out. |
| Jordi: | Son of a whore. [Again, *hijo de puta*, for the record.] |
| Leo: | Meet me in the ring. |

ON APRIL FOOL'S, a snowstorm blankets Montréal, a nasty joke played by the great trickster in the sky. After pacing my apartment all day, I venture into the streets feeling the exiled stranger in a film noir. Streetlights capture swirling snowflakes like dust in a labyrinth of concrete. Meanwhile, Buenos Aires lies inverted, below the equator, in an oppressively humid fall. It's absurd to think that spring and autumn can exist simultaneously, as truth and fiction do. To avoid sinking into a nostalgic funk, I wind up at the Spanish bookstore. Entering, I brush the snowflakes off the shoulders of my trench coat and see, near the door, a freshly translated stack of Lily Metterling's novel, *¡Hombre!* I pick up the book and discover, on the back of the dust jacket, effusive blurbs by her two macho idiots.

# RASPUTIN RED

"TITLES, LAZARUS. Pronto!" Jean Francois tosses him a packet of index cards.

"I've given you the titles. They're on the back of each canvas."

"*Red on Black* won't sell. Get personal."

"You've heard of Rothko?"

Jean Francois picks up his phone and starts talking to someone, his tone softer, more polite. A client, probably.

Lazarus walks to the desk in a corner of the gallery where an intern usually sits. He finds a red pen and counts out thirteen cards. He stacks them, pen poised, and stares at the inert ceiling fan and beyond, the exposed brick wall like Rothko's *Brown on Red*, satisfyingly linear with space to project one's own emotions. He shoots a glance at Jean Francois schmoozing on the phone. *Oblivion.* One down, twelve to go. He thinks of his parents. *The Defectors.* Thinks of himself. *Maladjusted.* There you go. He prints words on one card after the other. Two cards left. He thinks of his landlords. *Beholden.* Then the Japanese maple by their house. *Rasputin Red.*

Jean Francois flips through the cards. "Good. Except for the last one. No emotion." What? Rasputin Red rages with emotion. Lazarus shrugs. "It's all I've got."

"Work on it at home. Plus the last canvas you owe me, Lazarus. I need it pronto. A week Monday at the latest. Tuesday, we print the program and we'll be ready for the show. You'll have to tell me which title goes with which collage." Lazarus takes the cards, shuffles them, and drops them back on the desk. "Doesn't matter. Let your intern decide."

"We'll need some photos of you at work in your studio. I'll send a guy over next week."

Lazarus says he'll have to check with his landlords.

"The Planes? They're big fans of yours. They'll love the attention."

THE WALK BACK to his studio, though uphill, is easier than the walk down now that his portfolio's empty. Psychically, Lazarus always feels polluted after his meetings with Jean Francois. The man's aggressiveness and commitment to selling art make Lazarus feel tarnished. He should be grateful that the Saint-Henri gallery is giving him a solo show. Gratitude is hard to sustain. In the end, whatever help he gets, it's still just the precarity of him and his work. He's never satisfied. This stage, the letting go before a show, is the worst of his struggles.

Lazarus walks up Atwater. Graffiti on the concrete supports of an overpass shows a massive eye, blue, staring back at him with an interesting collision of fascination and contempt. When he first arrived in Montréal, the city did appear to resemble an eye beneath the bulge of the mountain, the eyebrow. But, when he finally walked to the top of the mountain and saw the various neighbourhoods blinking in the twilight, each stretching wide beyond the four points of the compass, he revised his analogy. Montréal is like many eyes, an argus of sorts, depending on where you live. Sometimes the eyes are friendly, seductive even, other times cold and dismissive.

He turns left on Sherbrooke and snakes up the streets of Westmount, trying to breathe out the toxins of his interaction with Jean Francois. When he crests the hill in the park and crosses beneath the towering oaks, acorns crunching underfoot, he begins to feel himself again. Two squirrels are involved in a manic chase, a prelude to what he'll be doing all weekend. There's a scent of burning wood in the air, as if the affluent are already lighting fireplaces for the coming winter.

He approaches the Victorian house, a solid rectangle with neither the heft of a mansion nor the elegance of a villa. The lights in the Planes' kitchen illuminate his landlords' doings. He averts his eyes, hoping they do the same when looking into his studio over the garage adjacent to the house.

At the foot of the driveway, the Japanese maple stands gracefully aloof from the structures. Lazarus stoops to collect a fallen leaf. Perfectly formed with seven lobes, the leaf lies on his palm like a single flame. He climbs the stairs, unlocks the door, and presses the leaf inside his thickest art book, the Miró.

Less than a minute later, some tap-tapping on his door and Kate Plane stands there, in her doorway, tightly wrapped in black Lycra. The tips of the maple down below are visible just above her head, as if her hair is on fire. "We're having a brunch, Laz, tomorrow. Can you come?"

It's her third invitation in as many weeks, which is how long he's occupied their apartment. Something perverse propelled him to decline her previous offers, but he's run out of excuses. They'll see him in his studio, knowing he's turned them down after all their generosity.

"Yes, thank you. I'll come."

Kate Plane smiles. "Wanna go for a run with me?"

Lazarus does not.

KATE PLANE waits outside while he changes quickly. They set out along Westmount Avenue, toward the mountain. Lazarus restrains his pace to accommodate hers. At first, she says little, but after a few blocks, she starts talking about her kid, her husband, details of their lives and routine. He's worried she'll expect a reciprocal amount of sharing from his end. It's too dark to take the steps up to the entrance of Mont Royal, so they loop back down a street toward Murray Hill Park. She stops at a water fountain while Lazarus jogs on the spot, trying not to look at her perfectly shaped legs, staring instead at the red leaves dangling off a maple.

"What are you thinking?" she asks, joining him on the path again.

"About red. Rasputin Red, to be precise."

"Who was he again?"

He tells her about the last Tsarina and her bizarre relations with Rasputin, the crazy mystic. "They had an affair and his influence helped bring down Imperialist Russia."

Rasputin, he explains, was born a Russian peasant and became a pilgrim, wandering from cloister to cloister, obsessed by religion. He had the gift of explaining the Bible to largely illiterate Russians as tales they could understand. Considered a healer, he was invited to the Tsar's palace in 1907. The Tsarina was frantic for her hemophiliac son and convinced herself that Rasputin's presence and his bizarre rituals could help Alexei. The so-called healer started spending a lot of time at the palace with the Tsarina and her family. In 1915, when Nicholas left Petrograd for the First World War's eastern front, Rasputin exerted his influence in the vacuum left behind. This only exacerbated the royal family's increasing unpopularity. Just before the February Revolution of 1917, Rasputin was assassinated.

"The details are murky, but it's thought that Rasputin was poisoned and dumped in the Neva River. His murderers were so incompetent, the corpse was soon found. Rasputin was then buried in an Orthodox cemetery, but later, his body was exhumed. Finally, they poured gasoline over him and burned the body. It took a lot of work to get rid of him."

"The Tsarina jumped off a train, right?" Kate asks. "In a snowstorm."

Lazarus could scream with laughter. "No, that was Anna Karenina."


HE WORKS UNTIL well after midnight then falls to the floor and does forty push-ups to warm up. Afterward, he crawls under his duvet. The studio, so bright by day, is a little too dark at night for his liking, and cold too. The concrete garage below gives off a frigid dampness that permeates into the space taken up by his canvases, paints, tools, and bed.

Trees creak in the wind and the occasional car rolls by. Next door, all is quiet. The Planes went to bed early. Or maybe their house is better insulated than this detached structure, the wooden studio built as an afterthought on top of the garage and described as "our mother-in-law apartment" by Kate when all this began. "We'd love to have an artist living there." Hard to say no, the place was rent-free and clean compared to his former dive in Barcelona. But the days are getting colder and he'll have to find a way to make it workable through the winter.

After a few hours of sleep, Lazarus boils some water and drinks coffee, pacing in front of the collage. It's lacking symmetry and cohesion. He shakes a cylinder of red paint and starts spraying. A red eye, then the words *burning soul.* He should be showering and dressing but gets carried away spraying over the leaves he pressed onto the plywood, pasting images and photographs until, shockingly, it's almost noon. Lazarus washes his red-spattered hands, grabs a clean blue shirt, and finds a bottle of cognac he received for his birthday from Elena.

Down his stairs to the driveway and up the main house's back steps, these ones freshly painted. He tries knocking. Laughter and voices inside. Should he have gone to the front door? He knocks again, and a woman opens the door. He's seen her leaving and entering the house. She's slightly stooped with a long black braid.

The kitchen is warm and smells of melting cheese. Lazarus rubs his hands over the stove to warm them up. Trevor Plane appears, carrying an empty platter. "Claudia, more salmon, quick, quick." He spots his tenant. "Lazarus, you made it! Get stuck in traffic or something? Ha, ha!" They shake hands, Trevor grabbing his arm like a politician. "Whoa, serious biceps." He's happy about the cognac, promises some good cigars after brunch, and hands Lazarus a plate of quartered lemons. "Take this, will you?"

Trevor leads the way into the dining room. The four other guests are already seated at the long table. Kate blows him a kiss from her place at the head. With her hair pulled back, she looks more severe, and tired too.

"This, my friends, is the artist we've been telling you about. Lazarus, our talent in residence." Kate points at each of the guests, listing their names far too quickly, then gestures to the empty chair to her left. "Sit!"

The conversations continue around him. Lazarus sips champagne, accepts smoked salmon and bread. Across from him, on the hutch, the collage the Planes purchased leans against the wall, as if they haven't quite decided what to do with it. It's one of his starker works and clashes with the pastel flowers of the wallpaper. In the central image, a dark-haired woman reclines on a sofa as a bomb detonates overhead. Along the borders, scraps of sheet music, burned at the edges, curl off the canvas.

The food helps calm Lazarus. These people are talkers, which relieves him of having to come up with anything clever of his own. Next to him, a woman is going on about a movie he hasn't seen, but he nods along until Kate turns to him. "I don't know. Let's ask him. What's your real name? I mean, you go by the single name, like Cher." She laughs tightly. "But you're what exactly, from where?"

"Didn't you ask him before letting him stay here?" the woman next to him inquires.

"We just fell in love with him, right Trev?"

Trevor, at the opposite end of the table, launches into a description of their first encounter with Lazarus, last month at a vernissage near the old port. How they "discovered" the artist and, on learning of his "difficult circumstances," were more than glad to offer the empty space over the garage. "We always thought it would be an excellent studio for an artist. And better than having to put up with a mother-in-law next door, right Kate?"

Laughter, then a pause, and the woman next to him, Suzanne apparently but called Suze by her friends, regards him with raised eyebrows. "Really, who are you?"

"I make collages."

"How old are you?" Kate asks.

"Thirty."

"Wow. I thought you were older."

He hopes that's enough information for now.

"Go on," Kate says.

"My parents were Russian. They died when I was quite young." Jean Francois has told Lazarus to play down parts of his bio, play up others. It's like participating in his own erasure, but he skips the part about growing up in Vermont, studying art at Bennington. "I went to Paris when I was twenty-one. I spent some years there, then lived in Barcelona before coming here."

"What part of Russia?" someone asks.

"My parents were born in Saint Petersburg, back when it was still Leningrad." He notices the bodies tighten, unconsciously perhaps. These people came of age during the Cold War of Ronald Reagan, when Russians were still the bad guys. Lazarus adds, "The city's evolving names reflects its citizens' identity crises."

The attempted joke is met with blank stares. Lazarus summarizes the name changes, from Saint Petersburg to Petrograd, in 1914, then Leningrad, in 1924, and back to Saint Petersburg, in 1991.

"And your name?" Suze askes.

"I was baptized Danius Lazahr, but early on, I opted for the one name." Lazarus doesn't bother with the story told by his mother, how she'd looked at her newborn one afternoon in Vermont and decided to call him Lazarus, proclaiming "This baby never smiles!" The Planes wouldn't know the Orthodox interpretation of the myth of Lazarus. That, after being resurrected from death by Jesus, Lazarus never once smiled in his remaining thirty years. He'd been too traumatized by the tortured, unredeemed souls he'd witnessed during his four days in Hades. Sometimes Lazarus could believe that, embedded in his genetic memory, was hell witnessed first-hand.

He also left out the parts about his father's seniority in the Soviet bureaucracy and how his mother convinced him to follow Solzhenitsyn to Vermont, where they lived a few kilometres away, in Dorset, without ever meeting the dissident ensconced behind the barbed-wire fencing of his farm.

"Baptized? So, you're what, Russian orthodox?"

"Not really. My father was an atheist." How little these people understood Eastern European complexities, the intermarriages and survival tactics during revolutions, occupations, and war. His maternal grandmother was a Jewish aristocrat, and that very collage in the Planes' dining room was inspired by her courage during the German occupation. "We're a mix of everything."

"Like a collage, right?" Kate takes his hand on the table and squeezes it. Maybe she feels entitled after catching him staring at her legs on their run, or maybe she picks up on the grief between the lines of his story.

"Whatever you are, we like you very much, Lazarus, and your collages too." She points to the one on the hutch. "He knows a lot about art. Tell us, the same way you explained collage at the gallery when we met you."

"Collage," Lazarus says, "is the term used for the *papier collé* that emerged out of the Cubist movement when Braque and Picasso played with textures and geometries." And he tells them how, as early as 1908, Picasso created *Le Rêve*, a figurative drawing on which he pasted a small piece of paper, a painting within a painting, of a ship, suggesting imaginary travel. This three-dimensional exploration led to the applications of newspapers, restaurant menus, and photographs to act as real themes in counterpoint to the abstract structure depicted in paint on the canvas. "The artists were asking, 'What is illusion and what is reality?'"

Lazarus stops there. All he's given them is the modern history of western collage. Invoking Picasso catches the attention of potential collectors. But the tradition of collage is as old as the inventions of paper in Mesopotamia, Egypt, and China. In the tenth century, Japanese calligraphers applied glued paper to the works containing their poems.

"Tell them about Barcelona and why you came here."

He skips the part about his love affair with a Catalan woman and mentions Miró's collages, how he was drawn by their wild humour and fantasy, the abstract surrealism of their organic shapes. "I went to Barcelona to study his work. And then, just before the financial crisis, the Catalan government organized an exchange program with Québec. A few weeks after I got here, the program was cancelled."

Claudia serves plates of eggs benedict and the conversation drifts elsewhere. There are salads, cheeses, and grapes. Lazarus eats and eats. These couples with their abbreviated names, Mel and Suze, Bret and Irey, they know one another well and speak in a shorthand that's largely incomprehensible to Lazarus. When he feels sufficiently stuffed, he puts down his fork and asks Kate where her daughter is. "Jessie's at a sleepover, thank God."

Lazarus would have liked to see the girl. Whenever he runs into her, usually when she's entering or leaving one of the Planes' garages accompanied by a nanny, she seems unusually silent given her gregarious parents. He would like to give Jessie some paper in his studio and see what she'd do with watercolours and felt pens. Maybe Jessie's drawings would help him understand this family. It surprises him that he even cares. Perhaps he misses his own loud, messy family more than he dares to admit. This is the closest he's lived to a surrogate version in a long time.

The phone rings from various locations in the house. Claudia emerges from the kitchen. "It's for you, señora. An emergency."

Kate sighs and takes the phone. She asks a few curt questions. "Okay then, you go and keep us posted." She puts down the phone. "My mother's had a stroke apparently. One of her caregivers will accompany her to the hospital."

Lazarus wonders whether he should leave. "No way," Trevor says, standing up and going for the bottle of cognac on the hutch. "Time for cigars, boys!"

Kate waves them off. "Suze and Irey, you stay down here with me. We've got that fundraiser to plan."

Lazarus follows the men up the stairs, through a family room with toys and a massive TV and outside, onto a small deck overlooking the back garden. Trevor switches on a shiny artificial fireplace that quickly warms the space. Lazarus takes a snifter and a cigar, lets Trevor light it up, and then sits down between Mel and Bret.

Trevor leans against the railing, snifter in the same hand as his cigar. He's tall and blond, the afternoon light playing in his hair as he talks about his work. The smoke hangs over the deck like a layer of gauze.

At first, Lazarus listens carefully, having wondered what this man does for a living. Kate, he knows, is a lawyer by training but now runs some kind of business foundation. It emerges that Trevor is a venture capitalist and spends his time scouring the globe for new start-ups. This explains why Lazarus so seldom sees him. Trevor is "on the road," he claims, five days a week, managing investments and finding new ones.

The three men discuss some deal in the offing. Mel's a lawyer whose advice Trevor seeks from time to time while Bret's the family accountant. Lazarus looks out toward the dazzling trees, their yellow leaves dancing against the cobalt sky. Nature so beautifully creates this perfect collage in motion and he has to wonder why he even tries.

Then he notices how visible his studio is from this angle. The garage and his space lie slightly lower and to the left. Some windows act as mirrors, reflecting the viewer's perspective, but the windows of his studio are transparent, exposing the interior even in broad daylight. Through them, he can see the collage he's been working on.

As is often the case with his larger works, distance reveals flaws. Not enough contrast among the images, the flames he painted on the sides of the plywood are too feeble, the outlines of the maple leaves too lacy. He sits there, staring into his studio, thinking about the work and that the Planes can see him at all times, that he absolutely has to get curtains for the three windows. Also some form of heating. This fake fireplace would be ideal.

"Hand me your phone."

Startled, he looks up at Trevor's extended hand.

Lazarus digs into his pocket and pulls out his cellphone, an old Nokia he bought in Barcelona years ago.

"You don't have a smartphone?"

Lazarus shakes his head and slides the phone back into his pocket.

"I'll demonstrate with mine." They butt out the cigars and follow Trevor into the family room. He dims the lights and connects his iPhone to a palm-sized gadget. "Get a load of this. All wireless."

Projected on a white wall, taking up a good one by two metres, are the figures of two people on horseback, riding along a country lane. Lazarus recognizes Kate's hair streaming from her riding helmet and guesses that the small figure is Jessie.

"I filmed this last summer," Trevor says. "Look how great the projection is."

Lazarus can't see the faces, just the straight backs of the riders as the two trot away from the camera into a tunnel formed by the leafy branches of trees. The scene evokes space, dimension, and distance, elements he plays with in his work to develop a visual vocabulary of movement.

"This, my friends, is a breakthrough," Trevor is saying. "The projection is crystal clear."

The clip lasts two minutes, if that. Trevor replays it while promoting the gadget and its compatibility with any device, a smartphone, tablet, or laptop.

To the soundtrack of Trevor's pitch, Lazarus absorbs the nuanced greens and blues of the scene, the imaginary lifeline between mother and daughter, the nobility and grace of the moving horses. You can fall in love with an image, not only for its beauty but for its possibilities. If he could make a collage of clips and project them from many devices with these gadgets, that would be a real breakthrough. But expensive, unless the gallery owner covers the cost. And who would buy such a digitized collage? The Planes, maybe, but how many Planes are out there? That depended on chance, and Lazarus does not consider himself naturally lucky.

Before they return downstairs, Lazarus asks to see the clip again but against another wall, one with shelving, books, and vases. Superimposed on objects, the scene appears dreamlike, a hallucination recontextualized on a bookshelf. A form of photomontage with an anarchy evoking the Dadaists. Arp's collages of the thirties with their *papiers déchirés* expressed his torment and delusions, bringing him closer in his mad search for unattainable perfection.

IN THE LIVING ROOM, Kate and the other two women are sitting on the sofa and armchairs, drinking coffee. Behind them, a baby grand piano displays silver framed photos of the family. Lazarus remains standing, hoping for an exit strategy. Surely

Kate is worried about her mother. But there's no mention of the stroke or the need to rush to hospital. Lazarus stares at the piano. He hasn't played in a while and misses it. Kate catches him out. "You want to play it, don't you?"

"No, it's fine. I should be—"

"Please play something." Kate's face softens, or maybe he sees her differently after viewing her ride on horseback into a mysterious tunnel.

Lazarus opens the keyboard and plays some Bach. His fingering's a little rusty, but he manages to get through the piece. Amazing how much memory resides in the hands. Your brain thinks it's forgotten, but the muscles remember. Then he plays a tune by Arvo Pärt, gets lost in the complexity of the piece, doesn't sense her presence until he catches a whiff of jasmine. Kate places a hand on his shoulder. He can't play that way, not with her weight against him. Lazarus gets up, says his goodbyes and thank-yous. Glancing just once at her eyes, he sees their grey fragility.

IN THE DAYS following the brunch, Lazarus settles into an austere schedule that revolves solely around his work. Get up early, go for a run, shower, have coffee, and work until sunset, which occurs earlier every October day. He likes the mania of this approach, imposed by the deadline of the show's opening. One afternoon, he walks down to the mall on Atwater and buys three space heaters and two extension cords at the Canadian Tire.

Occasionally, Lazarus spots the Planes arriving or leaving in their cars. On a Friday evening, he's out for a quick walk to clear his mind. Trevor steps out of a limousine. They talk for a moment. Lazarus feels obliged to ask how the latest trip has gone, and the man shakes his head. "A tough one. We had to implement a round of layoffs in one of our tech investments. A solar panel producer, totally unprofitable. We've made the managers outsource everything." He describes calling the employees into a conference room and handing out a sheet of paper listing the names of those let go.

"There's no nice way, Lazarus. Like a Band-Aid, you rip it off quickly. Well, you saw enough of that in Spain, I guess. But there, the people get unemployment cheques or early retirement. That's the Euro zone for you." Then he thanks the artist. "I'm grateful to you, pal. Keeping an eye on the family while I'm on the road. It's, you know, reassuring." He punches Lazarus lightly on the arm and walks to the front door.

That encounter sticks in Lazarus' mind. Not the part about keeping an eye on the family but the part about the layoffs. The brutality of it. Trevor didn't enjoy the job of laying people off, but he did not hesitate to inflict pain.

That night, it's cold outside but warm enough in the studio thanks to the space heaters. Lazarus works by the windows, his collage in progress illuminated by second-hand lamps he set up to improve the lighting. Sometimes he stops and looks up quickly toward the deck where he smoked the cigar with Trevor. There's a movement of the curtains, as if someone is stepping back from the window. Jessie, most likely, or her nanny or Claudia, he tells himself. But, deep down, he senses that it's Kate.

On his runs, he thinks about the image of the woman and daughter riding into a tunnel formed by the outlines of Japanese maple leaves, their fiery reds building on the theme of his last collage. He's still not satisfied with the work.

Elena calls to check in on him. She's a textile artist, and while they're talking, he asks if she has any bolts of fabric he could use for curtains. "Sure, I've got this humungous piece that would be perfect. Kind of like parachute material. Synthetic, for sure, but it'll work well."

The next day, Elena drives over to the studio in her pickup. He helps her carry the bolt up the stairs. She enters his studio, throws her coat on the bed, rolls up the sleeves of her baggy white shirt, and puts her thick hair up into a bun. He likes the energy she brings to the studio. Elena tells him to hammer a row of long nails into the tops of the window frames, not all the way but leaving a good two inches sticking out. Then she shows him how to loop the fabric over the nails without having to make a single cut in the cloth. White gossamer folds cover the windows, allowing the natural light in but making him feel less exposed.

It's snowing outside. When they finish, there's a mechanical racket from the driveway. Elena looks out the window. "Two snow blowers and a guy shovelling snow off the steps."

Lazarus pushes back a swath of the shiny fabric. "I'm not surprised."

Elena probes and he explains how his benefactors seemed to employ a small army of people to cook, drive them, care for their daughter and parents.

"I bet they even outsource sex!" Elena laughs.

Lazarus opens a bottle of wine and they eat some cheese and bread, sitting on his floor in the fading light. He tells her about Trevor's gadget and how he'd love to use it to create and project moving collages. Elena whips out her camera. "I'll film you, right now, over there, against your new curtains."

Lazarus puts on some klezmer music and dances a crazy half-Russian dance, skipping barefoot across the floor, contorting his body, flailing his arms, kicking. A celebration, he feels, for this studio that's become his warm cocoon. He'll stay until spring, he thinks as he dances around, maybe even summer. Not paying rent means he can buy good paints and wood and work hard toward another show next fall. At which point, maybe he'll be able to afford his own space.

He twirls and dances, then trips over the spaghetti of wires around one of the extension cords and collapses on the floor. He takes Elena's hand and kisses it. She shivers and he kisses the tattoo on her forearm, a small infinity symbol in red. "Maybe we shouldn't," she says, but eventually they do. Lazarus wants this feeling he has, that he's not quite the nomad anymore, to last forever. Not often in his life has he allowed himself to imagine the future.

Lazarus makes coffee and then walks her down the stairs to the street, where she parked the pickup. A beautiful snowy glow shrouds the avenue. Elena starts the truck and drives off. The silent stars and winter moon hover over the city, an attainable perfection that strikes him as a precise expression of how he feels.

He hears the knocking just after hanging his coat on the hook by the door and opens it. Kate stands shivering in the doorway, wearing a pale-blue sweater and jeans. Her hair is loose and messy.

"What's wrong?"

"Nothing." She has a pen and a red booklet in her hand.

"Come in."

Kate looks around the studio, takes in the improvised

picnic on the floor, the unmade bed, the waves of fabric draping the windows. "We should really get you a table and some chairs."

"I don't need them. The space is fine." Lazarus guesses she doesn't really care about furniture. She wants to know what he's been doing now that she can't see him quite so clearly from her house.

Kate opens her book. It's an agenda with tiny handwriting scrawled on the pages. "I want you to teach Jessie to play piano."

"I'm not a—"

"She's been bugging me. Can you make Thursdays at four? After her skating lessons."

And, absurdly, because he has no intention of giving piano lessons to anyone, let alone Kate's daughter, he says, "Won't she be tired? I mean after the skating."

"Okay then, it's a deal."

"I'm sorry. No. But I tell you what. Now and then, Jessie can visit me here in the studio and I'll show her how to draw with charcoal or paint with watercolours."

Kate sits down on a cushion on the floor and flips through her agenda. "Next Thursday, the thirtieth. Wait. She's got a rehearsal in the school play. So, we'll make it seven, exceptionally."

She doesn't move from the cushion. He offers her coffee or leftover wine. She accepts a glass, takes a few sips. The wine leaves a red mustache on her upper lip. Lazarus sits down on the floor, his back to a space heater alongside the window. Sweat trickles down his spine.

"My mother died last week."

"I'm sorry." He wonders whether he should embrace her.

"One less thing to worry about." She drinks the wine in one long gulp. "You don't know anything about me."

This may be true, and if so, it's mutual.

"I watch you, Laz. You're driven. You know what you want. I envy that." Then she gets up. "I should go. Jessie's alone. Nanny's night off."

"Your husband's away?"

"He's always away."

She doesn't air-kiss him when she leaves, probably because she's smart enough to deduce that Lazarus wants her gone. Even if he hadn't made love to Elena, he would not want this woman. And she knows it. Lazarus fears the consequences.

He creeps under his duvet even though the heat in the studio feels subtropical. He falls asleep and dreams of torn fragments—postcards from Barcelona, the ripped remnants of a parachute, musical scores belonging to his grandmother— that form a visual biography of his life.

That night, he's shocked into wakefulness by a series of explosions. Flames leap from the curtains to his paints. There's no time to throw water. He crawls through the smoke, grabs his coat and the last collage he finished, and runs outside to call 911. Kate is already standing outside, her arm around Jessie. By the time the fire trucks arrive, the studio is engulfed in flames. Firefighters train their hoses on the garage and are able to save the cars. The water begins to freeze, strange conical patterns forming off the railings and roof of the studio. The Planes' house and the Japanese maple stand unscathed.

Lazarus loses his paints, his tools, and his few possessions. Some months later, as he's getting ready for his show to open, Jean Francois tells him the fire was the Planes' fault, that according to city regulations, the studio should have been equipped with a smoke detector and better wiring. Lazarus imagines they still blame him.

*Mad Humour in the Face of Disaster* opens on a Sunday afternoon. A cellist plays in the corner and waiters circulate with trays of prosecco while crowds of strangers orbit the collages. Feeling superfluous, Lazarus moves from group to group, accepting handshakes and compliments. At one point, the crowd parts and he spots two figures standing before the only collage he was able to save from the fire. The taller of the two is Kate, whom he hasn't seen since that fateful night. She rests her hand on her daughter's shoulder as they study his collage's fiery reds, charred wood, and foliage. He moves closer to them, listening.

"Yes, those are the leaves he took from our tree," he overhears her saying.

Perhaps sensing his presence, Kate turns and catches Lazarus eavesdropping. But then someone speaks to him. When he turns back again, the mother and daughter are gone.

# DON'T TELL PABLO

DRIVING IN dense traffic on a Friday afternoon in June is a lot like living. Everyone wants to get to the beach quickly and wrench out every potential second of long weekend festivities. All easily undermined by one misstep—a distracted second, an unseen red light, a flare-up of prideful testosterone. Such are Maggie's preoccupations as they stop to pick up the kid.

Pablo slides into the back seat, next to Maggie, and slips on his headphones, nodding in time to the music, hip-hop from what she can faintly discern.

Andrés swerves the Fiat back into traffic. As they snail-pace through Barcelona, Andrés and Havel chat away in the front, their Spanish too quick and truncated for Maggie to follow. The backs of their balding heads look flat, as if they spent too much time sleeping face up as babies. Another reason why motherhood puts her off. One false move and you've wrecked your child forever.

Maggie tries to look out for the beautiful features she's discovered in the city. How is it that some places produce more than their fair share of artists? Barcelona ranks right up there with Vienna, Paris, and Prague. Her own city isn't exactly shabby although Montréal doesn't have the same scale of ingenuity she's discovered here during the last two weeks. Maybe the massive mural of Leonard Cohen put up shortly after his death would qualify. His signature fedora and tender gaze loom over downtown Montréal as a giant hallelujah.

When the car passes the suburbs, Maggie points her phone out the window, captures some blurred shots of Serra de Montserrat, and then turns to Pablo. In profile, his long eyelashes curve in the daylight. She's tempted to take his photo but doesn't want to intrude on his space, especially considering that they just met and what she knows of his situation. Maggie remembers thirteen as the age she started to value—no, hoard—her privacy. He's still a boy, sturdy, compact, yet his head strikes her as close to the divine shape only the gods could have sculpted.

When they approach the Costa Brava, Andrés pulls the car into a gas station. Havel follows him to buy bottled water.

Maggie taps Pablo's arm. "What are you listening to?"

"A mix. You've heard of Migos? Childish Gambino? Musicians like those."

"That's why your English is so good."

"I guess."

Their conversation is interrupted by shouting and whoops of laughter as Andrés chases Havel around the car, spraying him with a water pistol.

"They grew up together in Argentina," Maggie says. "Whenever they see each other, they tend to regress."

"Guys do stuff like that. My father works in film. He likes

to play practical jokes on the actors." He looks down. "Or used to."

"Andrés told us about your father. It must be hard."

"I made him a strawberry *licuado* for lunch. He couldn't finish it, so I did."

Andrés jumps into the driver's seat. "Maggie, your lover's a lousy shot."

Maggie looks at Pablo and rolls her eyes. "Remember what I said about guys," he whispers and slips on his headphones.

She wonders if Pablo minds that she brought up his father's condition. Before picking the kid up, Andrés told Maggie and Havel that Pablo's father is dying of inoperable brain cancer. He asked them not to dwell on this in front of Pablo. "The kid needs a break from the bedside vigil."


ANDRÉS OPENS another bottle of Cava and the cork flies over the railing into the yard below. A tree of many lifetimes grows out of that arid spot, its branches extending past the terrace and over the rooftop of the beach house. Pablo occupies one end of the table, between two other teenagers, the children of Andrés and Cecilia. He's still wearing the same T-shirt, red with yellow piping, the colours of Catalonia, except now his lips and chin are oily from the paella he's devouring.

Maggie looks out at the tree and the man, a writer, at the table across from her. Luis owns the beach house and rents the upstairs to Cecilia and Andrés. He's old enough to be Maggie's father. Actually, he'd be older than her dead father would be today. An hour ago, when they first met, Luis's zany grin and white curly hair reminded her of Harpo Marx.

The sea breeze carries the drumbeats and guitar twangs of live music. Later there'll be dancing, a bonfire, and fireworks. The kids receive permission to check out the stage set up on the beach. Pablo kisses Cecilia in thanks for the meal and waves at Maggie, who peers over the terrace railing to watch them proceed down the street. Pablo rides his skateboard with acrobatic grace. Since arriving at the beach house, he seems determined to have fun. What is solstice if not the celebration of lingering light? Particularly if you live in a cold northern climate, Maggie thinks. She resolves to follow Pablo's lead.

As they finish eating the paella, Luis describes working on the script for Pablo's father's latest film. It's a tribute to the resilience of street kids in Barcelona during the Civil War. Orphaned by the bombings, the kids learn to live by their wits, finding shelter, stealing food, and making up games. Most of the cast are under eighteen and have never acted before. The film was shot and edited in the year preceding the filmmaker's diagnosis of brain cancer, his treatments of radiation and chemo.

Luis says Pablo's father doesn't believe he'll live to see the opening. "The film's dedicated to his son, but don't tell Pablo. He doesn't know."

Perhaps to cheer them up, Cecilia brings out a platter with the famous Sant Joan cake she purchased at the bakery in S'Agaró. After all the Cava and paella, the rectangle of saffron dough with dried fruit between layers of custard looks overwhelmingly large on the serving plate. Everyone stares at the cake until making a collective decision to save it for when they come back from the fireworks.

Maggie's impressed by their cooperative spirit. Her friends

at home would've argued longer, with someone insisting on eating the cake immediately. Maybe that's what war and bombings do to a place. At various times in history, such places have been reduced to rubble. It pulls people together. With rebuilding comes an indomitable creative spirit.

IN THE MORNING, still feeling the wooziness of too much Cava, Maggie accompanies Andrés to pick up croissants for breakfast. An aura of lethargy hangs over S'Agaró. The streets are strewn with streamers, party litter, and casings from the fireworks.

On the way back to the beach house, Andrés stops at a newsstand for smokes. Maggie waits for him in a shady corner. City workers are dismantling the stage by the beach in the shrill morning light.

Andrés runs toward her, flapping a newspaper in his hand. "Food poisoning from the Sant Joan cake!" he huffs. "At least 385 people have been hospitalized."

Inside the beach house, Andrés pounds the bedroom doors, waking up the occupants to interrogate them. Maggie goes to the kitchen. The cake is sitting in its platter on the counter, one fist-sized corner missing. A deadly mess of custard oozes from the incision.

Andrés stomps into the kitchen. "I don't know who ate that piece. Not the kids, not Cecilia, not you and Havel."

"What about Pablo?"

"What about me?" Pablo leans against the doorway, yawning. "Why'd you barge into our room like that?"

"I didn't see you, Pablo."

"I was sleeping on the floor."

"Did you have any cake?"

"That? Gross. Definitely not."

EARLY EVENING, they set off for a walk toward the red cliffs of S'Agaró. Pablo and the other two kids lead the way up the path by the sea, followed by Andrés and Havel. As the path narrows, Maggie walks behind Cecilia with Luis trailing the group.

Down below, white sails criss-cross the bay, the waters intensely blue-green. The specks on the horizon could be ships crowded with refugees. Maggie pauses to consider the juxtaposition of the dazzling vista on the ugliness of politics. How beauty is small and local, feels graspable, while fear is pervasive and large.

Luis catches up to her. To make up for his slow climb, he jokes about his constitution, "tougher than any saintly cake," and engages Maggie with questions about her and Havel's lives in Montréal and her impressions of Barcelona.

"What struck you in our city of marvels?"

"The Miró museum and the large panels. Each depicts the squiggly black outline of a brain containing varying slashes of colours, like red or yellow."

"*The Hope of a Condemned Man.* Painted during the dying days of Franco. Miró captures the stages of imminent death—fear, insane hope, redemption. But never surrender. There's such resistance!" Luis mentions Pablo's father. "You know he calls his son Pau. It means 'peace' in Catalan."

"Do you speak Catalan?"

"Yes, but badly." He sounds apologetic.

One last curve in the path and they reach the summit. The

others are sitting on the wall, their backs to the Mediterranean. She takes out her camera and approaches Pablo for a close-up. His red T-shirt, maybe his hair, smell of pot.

"How's it going, Pablo?"

"Awesome."

"You know what a martini shot is?"

"Shot, yes." Pablo cocks his thumb, points his index finger at the sky, and pulls the trigger.

"I bet your father knows. The martini shot's the last scene of the last day of filming a movie. The cast and crew go out to drink martinis after."

Pablo raises an invisible glass to his lips. Then he stands, takes the camera from her hand and swivels toward the sea.

"*Si, perfecto. Con la vista y todo.*"

He drops to one knee and takes her picture.


NEXT MORNING, Havel brings a cup of coffee to Maggie's bedside. His face is sober, tentative, like he's about to confess something awful.

"What is it?"

"They got the call just now. Pablo's father died."

"Poor Pablo."

"He doesn't know. Pablo's mother wants to tell him in person. The plan is for Luis to drive the boy back to Barcelona around noon."

Maggie doesn't want to collaborate in a morning of fakery. But she can't bring herself to abandon Pablo. Something about the kid and his gallantry. She finishes her coffee and heads down to the beach with Havel.

Pablo kicks a soccer ball around with some kids. Just before noon, he tosses his red T-shirt onto the sand by Maggie's feet and races into the water. Andrés and Havel follow, afraid to lose sight of him. They take turns flipping Pablo into the waves, showing him how to bodysurf back to the shore. Soon they're all walking upside down on their hands, legs kicking wildly in the air.

Havel comes out of the sea, waterlogged and tired. "He won't get out of the water." A faint honking on the street by the beach as Luis pulls up in his black sports car.

Cecilia tiptoes across the hot sand until she's standing ankle-deep in the surf. In the water, Pablo's sitting on Andrés's shoulders, riding him like a bull. Cecilia wades toward them, starts talking to Pablo.

Andrés leaves them, comes to dry off. "The kid won't stop playing. It's as if he knows."

"Sure he does," Maggie says. "One look at our faces."

Cecilia takes Pablo's hand and pulls him back to shore. He dries himself off and puts on his T-shirt. Then he says "*adiós*" and "*gracias*" to each of them, one by one. When he gets to Maggie, he gives her a high five.

Pablo insists on walking to the car alone. He crosses the sand with all the dignity of a young matador facing death. Maggie catches a last glimpse of red and yellow before the door closes and the car pulls away.

# UNDER THE JACARANDA

OFFICIALLY, NOBODY in the capital was dying that spring. Worse, business was disappearing just after the cemetery's first expansion in over a century.

In the stone cottage uphill from the gates, the morning ritual, a usually serene sharing of two *cortaditos* brewed in the little kitchen next to the office, became more anxious with each deathless day.

As the cemetery's administrator, Gabriel Seil blamed himself for not resisting the absentee owner's demand to increase fees. "We're priced out of the market," he said, mustering the authority of someone who'd studied economics instead of literature.

"Eh, señor, it's always quiet in October. Once Christmas comes, we'll be busy again." Castillo leaned against the windowsill, sunlight reflecting off his gold teeth.

Gabriel dug through the papers on his mahogany desk. "Somewhere I've got the fees charged by other cemeteries."

"Did you visit them yesterday?" Castillo hesitated to mention the mysterious mounds cropping up in the new lot, six acres yet to be graced by a single tombstone or mausoleum.

"I slipped into the Colonial around noon. No freshly dug graves, no hearses or any sign of activity. And the smaller cemeteries were all quiet too."

Castillo regarded the coffee grounds in his cup for a clue. How to keep his boss calm? All he saw was the shape of a tailless mongrel, like one of his but skinnier. He rinsed out the cups in the kitchen and drove his tractor to the new lot. The pomegranate trees and wild rose bushes required taming, and it was essential to appear occupied. Jobs were as scarce in Luscano as the Andean condor. The Cementerio Real was his home, as it was home to his three dogs.

Gabriel frittered the day on futile tasks. In between, he paced in the shade under the jacaranda tree in full purple bloom. *Carabineros* were hauling off innocents in the dead of night. Was it possible that the country's poison was infiltrating this pastoral refuge? He, too, had been corrupted, reduced to spying and laziness. Only Castillo was as pure as the blades and flowers he tended, digging holes for the smallest coffins with such devotion.

Before sundown, Gabriel descended the gravel road between sentinels of pines. Locking the cemetery gates behind him, he recalculated how long his savings would last if he lost his job. Two months' rent, the rest for food, and then what? He couldn't fathom returning to the bookstore, begging for his old job at a time when half the country's books were banned.

Gabriel dodged the traffic on Avenida Reconquista, a zigzag dance to frenzied honking and cursing. At the bus stop, he stood at the end of a weary line and hugged his briefcase to his chest. It was bulky with a new edition of *The Ingenious Gentleman Don Quixote of La Mancha*. He wasn't the type to pray in public, but what were the chances he could will a head-on collision to happen, a busload of passengers, an ice cream truck, some blameless bystanders. Twenty mangled bodies, no children of course. At least half would wind up at the Cementerio Real given their market share.

After sunset, Castillo finished his dish of rice. Switching on the light bulb over the screen door, he sat on the front steps of his shack with a knife and a sanded branch of cherrywood to carve a guitar player modelled after the weathered gaucho he'd seen at the market. The dogs sniffed at the rising mound of wood shavings on the ground. Whittling usually steadied him, but on this night, he couldn't chisel away his worries.

Late in the afternoon, he'd discovered new mounds of earth in the empty lot. How to inform the boss? The man was already nervous as a *carpincho*, the rodent who taunted the dogs from tunnels burrowed beneath Castillo's shack. In his anxiety, he overcarved the gaucho's bent legs.

He sat beneath the bare light bulb's glow, trying to reimagine the misshapen wood in his palm. One dog, then a second, began to growl. He stood up, hoping for Juanita to emerge from the shadows with a packet of empanadas. But the dogs knew his girlfriend well enough not to bark. At their insistence, Castillo followed them to the corner where suicides and ex-convicts lay in unconsecrated graves. On the other side of the stone wall, heavy footfalls receded on the pavement. Crickets and frogs crooned from the ditch, through the sweet smell of wild roses. The dogs coiled around his legs. Then he returned to his shack and tried to sleep.

THE MORNING ritual began with Gabriel handing him the morale-building *cortadito* with four sugars already well stirred. "I'm sure we'll get work today. Hope you're up to digging some graves."

Castillo wasn't even up to grinning. He described the homemade graves he'd seen on the lot and the two discovered this morning by the wall. "People are digging their own graves."

"Are you sure? Did you actually see a dead body?"

The administrator raised and dismissed various theories until Castillo proposed they spend the night under the jacaranda. Reluctant to resort to spying, Gabriel suggested they camp out in his office instead.

Castillo gently brought his boss around. "We'll be tempted to turn on the lights and they'll see us. Outside, we'll have full view of the grounds."

As usual, Castillo was right. The southern constellation and moonlight that night illuminated the sculpted marble of the elaborate tombs belonging to the rich. All around, ghostly reflections of crosses and graves undulated across the acres.

They spoke little so as not to reveal their presence. Gabriel read until it became too dark, then lay his head on *Don Quixote*, which he propped against the trunk of the tree. Castillo's practised eyes allowed him to fashion the magnificent wingspan of an Andean condor from what had once been a guitar. His knife gleamed in his hand, their only armament. Just as well, for Gabriel had never a held a gun. When a flower from the tree dropped on his head, he almost screamed out.

Finally the sky paled and horneros sang from the branches above them. The two men rose stiffly and descended the gravel road to unlock the gates. Halfway down, they spotted a pile of what appeared to be carpets. Nearing the gates, they discerned the heap of bodies rolled in burlap. Early traffic slithered by on the avenue.

"I'll get the tractor," said Castillo. "We load them onto the trailer, and then I'll start digging."

"How many are there?"

"I'm counting half a dozen."

"Any children?"

"No, señor."

"Should I call the *carabineros*?"

"For what?"

It was satisfyingly busy that day. Castillo planted the bodies beneath the pomegranates and whittled pine crosses for each grave. At Gabriel's request, the young Franciscan came in the afternoon to consecrate the dead. He spoke a psalm and Castillo handed out six sprigs of wild roses, which they scattered over the mounds. The flowers fell like soundless tears onto the humid earth.

No one ever came to claim the disappeared. When the heat of summer erupted with Christmas fiestas, official business picked up just as Castillo had predicted.

# HOTEL TANGO

THE TAXICAB swerves from the *autopista* and brakes into gridlock on the world's widest avenue. Gabriel's face smacks the front headrest. His body bounces in his seat, his head thrown back. No seatbelts in the cab, of course. Just his luck to get a taxi driven by a gaucho. The manoeuvre strikes him as a warning. It's not appropriate to be visiting the metropolis right now. Then again, so little about Gabriel's relationship with Aude is appropriate.

Noon on Monday, and Avenida 9 de Julio has immobilized into a sixteen-lane parking lot. The taxi edges forward half a block and the meter clicks two more pesos. Gabriel hears drumbeats and horns honking, then shouting and metallic clattering.

"What's happening?" he asks, rubbing his forehead.

"*Protestos.*" The reply uttered like a curse.

A crowd swarms the intersection. Women bang on pots with wooden spoons. There are students with banners and impoverished retirees trudging behind them. The type of scene

Gabriel witnessed at home on CNN Argentina. An eruption of outrage, *porteños* venting on the streets of their city.

Buenos Aires is a cauldron of chaos. Gabriel implored Aude, in numerous phone calls to Ottawa, to relocate their rendezvous. Montevideo, Rio, Santiago, anywhere but Argentina. Aude resisted. It must be Buenos Aires, she repeated.

The meter's rising exponentially and they're not even halfway to the San Telmo address sent in Aude's last letter.

"Can't we take a side street?" he asks. Just then, the cars surge forward and the driver accelerates. "Never mind," Gabriel mutters.

At the next intersection, another surge of protesters cross in front of the car. The driver sticks his head out the window and delivers a stream of invective. "*Hijos de puta, guachos, míralo al pelotudo...*"

A bald man stops to discern the source of the insults. Pivoting, he lifts a crowbar in his hands and brings it down on the taxicab, rocking the car and denting the hood. He takes off into the crowd, zigzagging between the cars on the avenue.

Gabriel tries to stop the raging taxi driver, but he's too slow. The driver leaps out and tears after the assailant, leaving the cab door open.

Now what? The crowd surges past the taxi, the light turns green and the cars behind the taxi are honking frantically. Gabriel grabs his bag, is about to make a run for it himself. Take the subway, get away from this mess. It occurs to him that Aude, too, may be somewhere in the traffic jam, and he hesitates.

The driver hops back in, doesn't even apologize, and accelerates toward San Telmo. As if to appease, he turns up the radio.

*Mi Buenos Aires querido…when I see you again, there'll be no sorrow or forgetting…*

The combined soundtrack of the driver's swearing and Carlos Gardel's tenor falsetto belting out his tango for Buenos Aires stirs something in Gabriel. A sense of convergence here in this city of glitter and action that renders his hometown a sleepy village by comparison. Castillo's omen, driving him early this morning to the airport outside Luscano, his gold teeth gleaming in the sunrise. With one arm relaxed on the pickup's open window, the other loosely navigating the steering wheel, Castillo asked, "Eh, señor, you're going to see your girlfriend, right? It'll be fine. Don't worry, I'll take care of the cemetery. Maybe she'll come back with you, eh?" Castillo always knows what Gabriel's thinking and tries to reassure him.

This time, it's more than just the prospect of seeing Aude for a whole week, the small favour she tosses his way on an annual basis. This time, he may have to beg, he may sound pathetic, but isn't pathos the source of anything deep? Strip away the cliché of the tango and the very form, its roots, reveal a pathos essential to the human condition, a resistance, and the heroic battle to survive.


*Ocho*. The number on the key she left for him at the reception. The number affixed in bronze to the door, three floors up. When she opens to his knocking, he finds her barefoot, hair wet, wrapped in a towel. Aude seems smaller, her head just skimming his shoulder. "Finally, finally," he says, dropping his bag on the floor.

Making love, their bodies slide and squirm, slick with

sweat. Gabriel's hands cannot linger on the softness of her flesh. It's Aude, her lemony smell, her face flushed and her eyes always open, gazing at him. Too hurried, he can't help it, and when he rolls off her, she asks, "What happened to your forehead? There's a red mark in the shape of a heart."

"Nothing," he says. "It's nothing."

"Yes, Gabriel, you are wearing your heart on your forehead."

I wish, he thinks. "Of course," he says.

Aude says she's exhausted from the eighteen-hour flight from Canada. As soon as she falls asleep, he studies her, trying to align the Aude of his memory with this real one. Her gaze always makes him feel vibrant. What does his gaze do to her?

When you don't see a beloved for a whole year, they morph in your mind, you fashion them into someone similar but different. Meanwhile, they change on their own, requiring a catching up. Aude looks a bit older, maybe, a few new lines creasing her eyes and lips. Still, almost fifty, she looks younger than her age. He, too, has changed, he's sure of it. I'm tired of waiting, of living for one week a year. At forty-two, his own aging is beginning to sink in, prompted by the discovery of white hairs in his dark curls, the sense that, when he looks in the mirror, his eyes seem greyer, his face more elongated. They never discussed their age difference. It's of no consequence.

Nor can he really articulate what he loves about her. Some strange combination of empathy and elusiveness, Aude's forthright curiosity, her voice. The English they speak together is inflected with her Norwegian cadences, the sounds of a fountain. She's also reserved. Sometimes her silence charms, other times it alarms. With her, Gabriel finds himself talking too much, as if he has to argue his way into her inaccessibility.

His friend Roma, the only person in Luscano who knows about Aude, often tells him that. "You want what you can't have, Gabriel. Seriously, you need to move on."

Gabriel takes a shower and inspects the room. It feels as improvised as the hotel itself, with Hotel Tango printed on the red awning outside the entrance. The reception area on the ground floor resembles a thinly disguised living room. The man who gave him the key was probably the owner, an older Argentine with dyed black hair and a formal demeanour. But it's really not a hotel, he concludes, more like a boarding house or a bed-and-breakfast with eight rooms. The garret smells musty despite the open window, as if the room is rarely rented out.

The narrow space is almost entirely taken up by the bed and a wardrobe, which he opens. Aude has unpacked her clothes, including a row of uncharacteristically bright dresses, red, black, light blue, and pink. He unzips his small overnight bag and hangs up his six shirts.

Gabriel smokes a cigarette, leaning out the window. Below, the Pasaje San Lorenzo is busy with afternoon traffic and pedestrians. He watches a couple leave the hotel, hears their conversation float up and disperse in the humid air.

The only thing really wrong with the room, he decides, after dropping the butt in the toilet, is the absence of air conditioning. He'll have to take a lot of showers.

She's lying there, lips parted, her body twitching. By the bed, he finds a guidebook she's left on the floor. Unnecessary, considering Gabriel knows the city well enough and has already formed a mental list of places he wants to show her.

He flips through the guidebook, finding Aude's notations

in the margins. In the section on San Telmo, she's underlined the tango lyrics: *Barrio de tango, moon and mystery...*

As early as 1806, he reads, British troops invaded the city during the war with Spain, duking it out *mano a mano* in the narrow streets. The covert and courageous resistance escalated into open counterattack. Women poured cauldrons of boiling oil and water from the rooftops, forcing the British to slink back to their ships.

Every city has its own brand of violence. Does Aude know that the earliest tangos were danced by men duelling with knives?

FOR THEIR FIRST meal together, Aude insists they go to a *tanguería* near the hotel, a vintage restaurant with high walls and panels of red velvet curtains. In the anteroom, where they wait for the maître d' to prepare their table, there's a gallery of black-and-white photographs. Three walls of literati, celebrities, and disgraced heads of state.

Aude lingers by the poets' portraits from the thirties, Jorge Luis Borges and Alfonsina Storni among them. Gabriel moves on to a photograph of Madonna from the late nineties, when she came to Buenos Aries to star in *Evita*. Not necessarily warmly received given the "get out Madonna" protests he read about at the time. Antonio Banderas, her co-star who played Che Guevara, is also featured, alongside Oliver Stone, one of the film's writers. Then there are photos of both Bushes, Bill Clinton, Henry Kissinger, and Augusto Pinochet.

He circles back to Aude. "Luscano isn't represented," he says, "even though so many of its heads of state went into exile here. It's always the case. Luscano's conveniently ignored as if we don't exist. Like we're some imaginary country."

Aude laughs. "You should not take it personally, Gabriel. Bolivia and Uruguay are not represented. Neither are Canada and Norway, for that matter."

At the table, the waiter brings two encyclopedia-sized menus. How can a restaurant offer so many dishes? The place is surprisingly packed considering the dire economy.

The wine relaxes him, as does Aude's smile when she lifts her glass. "To our week together," she says. "I love San Telmo, the little streets and old conventillos converted into studios and galleries. Let's go to the antique market tomorrow. After the lessons, yes?"

Gabriel isn't really interested in antiques or flea markets, but he nods before adding, "And the bookstores! There's one in Recoleta you have to see. It's a former theatre, all red and gold, several levels, and packed with books, lots of poetry no doubt, and a café where the stage used to be. Also, there's a bookstore in Palermo, Eterna Cadencia—near Borges's house, in fact." He's worried she's too focused on this one rather touristy barrio.

Soon, he's distracted by the pampa steak the waiter brings. The meat is served on a massive wood platter alongside roasted red peppers and potatoes. While they eat, Aude offers a sanitized update on her life in Ottawa, careful not to mention the husband.

"I have a job in a gallery," she says. "Part-time, but I like it very much. The space is rented out for functions and parties. When the parties end, we drink the leftover champagne."

Gabriel asks, "What kind of art?"

"It changes from artist to artist. Usually living, contemporary artists, mostly Canadian."

"You know," he says, "I'm unable to name a single Canadian painter."

This is when he'd like her to say, in her formal way, *Well you should come and visit and get to know Canadian art. I'll show you all the museums and galleries!* Instead, there's silence between them. Amid the din of voices from neighbouring tables, he realizes he's once again stumbled into a conversational cul de sac. To extricate himself, he tells her about the absurdity of featuring Evita and Che Guevara in the same drama because they had absolutely nothing to do with each other, and wouldn't it only be a foreigner to have come up with such an implausible scenario? He's rewarded with Aude's smile and the lights in her amber eyes.

Later, on the second bottle of wine, four musicians in tuxedos start playing on a stage at the back of the restaurant. Two violins, a piano, and a bandoneon. Old-style tango, but they're good. Only after he's ordered coffee does Gabriel think to ask, "What lessons?"


SEÑOR GRECO PACES before his audience of guests, who are seated in a prearranged semicircle of chairs. "Nearby, in the old port of Buenos Aires," he says, "the tango was born in the late 1800s. In the bars and alleys, proud men duelled to the rhythms of Africa."

Gabriel wills himself to tune out, ticking off the lesson on his mental list. One in progress, four to go. He should be savouring every second with Aude, but she's hijacked the agenda. No amount of pleading and begging in the tanguería last night or over breakfast this morning could shift her resolve. "I am certainly attending the lessons," she proclaimed. "You do not have to if, as you say, it will kill you."

The sarcasm in her voice overwhelmed his ability to convey to her why he loathed the idea of tango lessons. It's sinful, he now thinks, to participate in the commercialization of an art form best left to those who live and breathe the music. How would you like it, he should have said, if we went to Oslo and I made you take up Norwegian folk dancing? An imperfect analogy considering that Gabriel is not actually from Buenos Aires, but here he sits, squirming on a hard wooden chair, in the tango bar rented by the Grecos for the dance floor their lessons require, hating everything. His head throbbing and neck sore from the whiplash of yesterday's taxi ride.

He directs his loathing at the Grecos. Former schoolteachers, he learned over breakfast, who converted their home into the Hotel Tango. Now transformed into their version of a sexy couple. Señor Greco's wearing a glistening yellow shirt tucked into black pants. On his feet, buffed dancing shoes from the thirties. And the wife! From the dowdy presence in the breakfast room, she's squeezed herself into a shin-length sheath of cobalt satin with matching stilettos. Señora Greco presides over the boom box, the discs queued for the upcoming Torture Lessons.

"By the end of the century," Señor Greco continues, "the tango evolved into the kicks and flicks of the legs, the close embrace originating in the brothels." He demonstrates with a few fluid moves of his creased pant legs. "There you have it, the vocabulary of our tango. When you Europeans and Americans saw the dance performed in 1913, you were scandalized! Soon, the first wave of tango fever swept the world. My wife and I will now demonstrate the basic moves, then we'll take turns with each of you."

Gabriel sighs loudly. Aude shoots him a nasty glance. She's rapt, wearing one of the dresses, unsuitably pink and frothy. The other three couples are starting to get antsy. Two men from Rio, a French couple on their honeymoon, and a pair of older Americans from San Antonio fix their eyes on the Grecos. As if, Gabriel thinks, you can figure out how to dance the tango in a week.

A loud click and the scratchy strains of an early tango fill the bar. Señora Greco sidles to her husband and they dance slowly and deliberately on the hardwood floor. They're good, Gabriel has to admit, projecting the essence of the tango, a dance for those who have lived, maybe too hard, and lost much—jobs, wagers, friends, lovers. He glances at Aude, wondering whether he's in the process of losing her.

The Grecos part, the wife making a beeline for Gabriel, who submits to her clutches seeing how Aude is already in the arms of the husband. Of course, it has to be a tango about jealous love. Over his partner's shoulder, he watches Aude dancing smoothly while he's being dragged side to side, a kind of human metronome.

"Relax, rotate your hips...no, the other way." Señora Greco is trying to be gentle while he chokes from the intense perfume on her neck. "Don't jerk or look at your feet." And the coup de grâce: "Now hold me properly, like a man!"

He stumbles through the harmonies of violin and piano cavorting through the bar. After Señora Greco drops him like a hot empanada, the Texan woman, white hair coiffed into a shining helmet, throws herself at Gabriel. She assailed him over breakfast, having heard him speak to Aude in English, and demanded that he translate the lessons for her and her husband. Gabriel refused. "Just watch," he told her. "You'll be fine."

Well, she isn't fine, breathing heavily into his shoulder, stepping on his loafers. Aude dances with one of the men from Rio, both swivelling smoothly. As soon as the song ends, Gabriel dashes toward her and takes her hand. His feet shuffle, seemingly disconnected from his torso, as he tries to lead her through *Pensalo Bien*.

*Think hard*, the song warns, *before you take this step. Once you've taken it, there's no turning back.*

*Think hard because I've loved you so and you've thrown it all away.*

"Follow me, Aude." Gabriel leads her through the grand entrance of Chacarita Cemetery, the sun bearing down on his back. He's always admired this cemetery with more than professional interest. The scale of it, the long alleyways of tombs and mausolea. It doesn't feel as cramped as Recoleta Cemetery, where Evita's tomb draws long lines of tourists. Actually, Chacarita is quite deserted this afternoon, making it a perfect spot for an express kidnapping or robbery.

It's also risky bringing Aude to a place so closely associated with death. Gabriel is struggling to keep the mood upbeat after another morning of tango lessons. Two down, three to go. Aude resents his resistance and he resents her insistence. But, earlier, in the bookstore in Palermo, their moods lifted.

After dragging Gabriel to flea markets and artisanal shops catering to tourists, Aude went along with his plans for the day. He was relieved when she seemed to take to Palermo, its cafés and shops, hipsters crowding the terraces, the narrow streets and trees and edgy murals, the eternal conversations of porteños. The snippets of arguments he overheard—*she's the best guitarist.... Don't see that film, it's a disaster.... What the country needs is less military, more love....*

Inside Eterna Cadencia, they separated to browse the shelves and tables. Aude, as he knew she would, fixated on the poetry section. It was cleansing to find himself alone, picking up novels, putting them down, observing her from time to time, head bent over a collection, her lips mouthing the Spanish poems she was reading.

His hand hovered over a new edition of *Don Quixote*. So tempting but a little too pricey. Also on the heavy side. He reached for *El Tunél*, a slim book that, he'd read somewhere, was widely considered one of the world's best novels of the twentieth century. Sábato's dark masterpiece was in the tradition of *Zama* by Di Benedetto, which Gabriel *had* read, although the latter was far less known and acclaimed.

The difference between the two authors was their experience during the dictatorship. Di Benedetto was arrested, held for a year, tortured, and once in exile, unable to write much. Sábato lived to almost a hundred years old and, Gabriel recalled, headed up the Argentine truth commission into the disappeared after the fall of the dictatorship.

Intrigued by the opening epigraph—*In any case, there was a single tunnel, dark and lonely: mine*—Gabriel paid for the book and waited for Aude in the adjacent café, drinking his fourth coffee of the day.

When she joined him, Aude seemed happy, both of them leaving the bookstore with parcels of books that weighed them down along with the bags of takeout Gabriel purchased for their picnic in the cemetery.

Now, as they enter Chacarita, Gabriel leads her to the famous tomb located at the end of the alley. Set in the corner of two white walls of plaster covered with plaques from countries all over the world, there's a larger-than-life statue of the man's head on a pedestal, where his name is etched in dark lettering. Someone has slid a cigarette between the singer's lips. Heaps of fresh and fading bouquets of flowers lie along the base of the walls.

"Look, Gabriel, there's a plaque from Norway! Was Carlos Gardel that famous?"

"He was so popular that when he died, a woman in Cuba committed suicide and another in New York tried to poison herself. They called him El Zorzal Criollo and the songbird of Argentina."

"How did he die? He was only forty-five."

"His plane crashed in Medellín, Colombia, in 1935."

Gabriel sits down on a bench and smokes a cigarette, watching Aude move with grace, the folds of her yellow sundress flickering in the sun, as radiant as the day he first spotted her at a bookstore in downtown Luscano. Aude spoke to him first, asking if he'd read the book she was holding, an anthology of Luscanan poetry. Luckily, he had. They continued talking at a nearby café, and for once in his life, he felt like an extrovert. Two nights later, they met for dinner. Afterward, in her apartment, they sat on her terrace, ate oranges, and kissed to the sounds of waves breaking on the beach below. And that was how he thought of Aude, the figure of a candle, narrow, her head a flame, water always nearby threatening to extinguish everything that drew her to him.

Five years of slow, sporadic communications between annual visits ground him down. Time was running out for Gabriel, but he couldn't fathom begging her to come back to Luscano. This morning's tango had twisted into him like a dagger: *I don't want anyone to imagine the bitterness and depth of my eternal solitude.*

He unpacks the lunch and sets the food on the bench. Several *triples*, those marvellous Argentine sandwiches with hearts of palm, tomatoes, and cheese, thinly sliced between three layers of bread.

"Look at this!" She's pointing to a cardboard sign printed in blue crayon. *Gardel may be dead but he sings better every day....*


THE WHITE PORCELAIN dish of soup sits atop an oval glass fishbowl the size of a soccer ball. Inside, a goldfish circles frantically. Aude is delighted, lifting spoonful after spoonful of gazpacho to her lips, apparently seduced by the brouhaha evoked by the svelte waiter's presentation of her dish. The fish regards Gabriel, sending him telepathic calls for help, trapped inside an infinite loop of distress.

This is the kind of restaurant that relies on props to serve its food, a form of fakery in Gabriel's mind. Food as entertainment. Cringing at the prices on the menu, he'd passed on a first course, eating bread instead while knocking back gulps of the Mendoza Syrah.

From the dark shadows of the terrace, a boy emerges. Five, maybe six years old, he approaches their table and points at their breadbasket, eyes darting toward the restaurant.

"Just ignore him, Aude."

"I can't. Look how skinny he is." She takes her napkin and wraps the remaining bread. "Why is he out alone so late?"

Gabriel looks into the shadows. There are others squatting beneath a tree. "He's not alone, Aude." Then he feels for his wallet. It would be a disaster to lose it now, the wad of pesos he saved up getting thinner by the day. In Luscano, he's often approached by children asking for food or money. He has his regulars, whom he feeds and gives money to when he's eating pizza at La Loca, knowing they won't rob him. But, here in Recoleta, the district that dazzles with the glitz of fashionistas immune to economic crises, they're targets, especially Aude.

The boy sidles to the table. His eyes, almost black, reflect the sparkling lights strung over the terrace. Aude hands him the bundle of bread, then rummages in her purse.

Gabriel watches the kid. "*Hola. Qué tal?*"

The boy's eyes are on Aude, but he answers. "*Bien.*"

My question was stupid, Gabriel thinks. But the one syllable answer, delivered in a tone so matter of fact, touches him. Also, the boy's courage. This is the kind of place where diners are prone to insulting, kicking kids in the pants, or calling the waiter and getting them to dispose of the inconvenience.

The boy thanks Aude and retreats into the shadows of a jacaranda tree. Moments later, Gabriel sees him walking next to a woman with two other little ones, all of them carrying plastic bags stuffed with scavenged goods.

Aude finishes her gazpacho and the waiter removes the

fishbowl. Gabriel wonders what they'll do with the goldfish later, after the restaurant closes and the unfortunate creature is no longer needed.

"That rarely happened when I was living in Luscano," Aude says. "I don't remember very many beggars."

"The last five years have been rough," Gabriel says. He's not surprised that she has no clue.

"What's happening here?"

Where to start. "Aude," he says. "Every night, hundreds of thousands, maybe millions of people descend into the streets of Buenos Aires to scavenge. They're looking for food. Many of them lost their jobs in this crisis. Bank accounts are frozen, factories have been abandoned by the owners. Long lineups outside the embassies—"

"Yes, Gabriel, I know about the economic disaster. The Grecos are teachers, but they could not survive on their paycheques. They converted their home to a hotel to teach tango. I am thinking about the little boy. I could have done more. Buttered the bread, taken him inside the restaurant to the washroom to clean him up, or given his mother more money."

All the while, he's thinking, what would happen if I lose my job? The cemetery could carry on with Castillo. Without the work, I can't travel to meet Aude once a year. What then?

Aude is telling him about the soup kitchens in Ottawa that feed the homeless and deliver warm clothes and sleeping bags to huddled figures on cold winter nights.

He's trying to remind himself just what it is he loves about her. The real Aude, not the idea of her he's fabricated over the years, from a distance. Her intelligence and reserve. The fact that she reads only poetry, perplexing yet appealing. Her words, too, are always compressed. She's lived a sheltered life, in Norway, Luscano, Ottawa, focused inward. Not necessarily happily but flickering with light. Is there even any room for Gabriel in the verses she contemplates? Does she think of him when she's reading her Storni and Borges, her Dickinson and Carson? His thoughts spiral down in an infinite loop.

Just this morning, she danced with him to one of the few protest tangos. Had she not heard the words? *What is happening in this country? My God, we've sunk so low.... How angry I am to see so much injustice to humanity.*

AFTER THEY LEAVE Recoleta, Gabriel stops at a wine store near the hotel. He picks the same red he was drinking in the restaurant (half the price) and a bottle of champagne for Saturday, their last night together. The week is slipping by and there's so much he has to resolve. What if she doesn't want to resolve anything? He'll have to find the words.

He opens the wine in their hotel room and leans out the window for a smoke while she's in the bathroom. Someone's yelling in the distance, and he imagines the Grecos having an argument. He's almost jealous of their passion, a couple that has been together so long and can still dance the tango with more than a semblance of desire.

Aude lies down on the bed. He drops the butt into the toilet then offers her a glass of wine. She shakes her head, pats the space in the bed beside her. He knows he needs to shower, brush his teeth, but to hell with it. He takes off all his clothes and lies on top of her. She shimmies out of her nightgown. He holds her breast, small, alert to his touch, kisses her mouth, neck, shoulder, feels the heat of her body while she watches him with such gravity.

Angry sex is good, he thinks. It's real. It closes the distance. He tells himself her resistance is part of her game to ramp things up.

"Slow down," she says.

But he sits up, lifts her legs, drives into her, unstoppable. Then he flips her over, slides into her again. Aude is moaning. He comes and collapses onto her back.


"I'M NOT GOING," Gabriel says.

Aude doesn't even try to convince him. She sets off for her fourth tango lesson in the red dress with the plunging neckline. Gabriel drinks water from the tap, not a good idea given the age of the pipes and the iffy water supply, but his mouth is dry and his head throbs. He gets back in bed, tries to sleep, can't. He starts reading *El Túnel*.

He's almost finished the novel when he thinks of checking his watch. Where is she? The lessons usually end by eleven. Gabriel stands in the shower stall, soaping and rinsing, soaping and rinsing. Trying to wash off the delusional narrative of the novel. The confessions of a man, a painter, in jail for murdering his beloved. The infinite loop of the narrator's obsession from first meeting Maria at an art gallery to their secret rendezvous behind her blind husband's back. The deterioration of the narrator's state of mind as he convinces himself that Maria is disloyal to him as well, that she's also secretly sleeping with others. How he leaves their tryst, mails her a letter, changes his mind, tries to get the postal clerk to retrieve it, and when that doesn't work, decides to let fate run its course. He breaks down, goes back to see her, accuses Maria of leaving him all alone in the world, kills her in a fit of rage, and then goes to confront the husband, who knew all along about the clandestine relationship. Finally, the narrator turns himself in to the police for the murder.

Drying himself off, Gabriel faces up to the novel's message, transmitted via the narrator with whom he irrationally identifies. If he doesn't reign in his resentment, it could lead him to commit all manner of horrible acts. Not as far as murder but an undermining of any desire Aude may have for him. Last night's lovemaking, for example. Not rough but angry. She probably felt hurt.

Every time he sees Aude, he realizes how little he really knows her. They had only one month together before she left to rejoin her husband, in Ottawa. Her husband's posting in Luscano came to an end, and Aude lingered to liquidate the apartment. Gabriel tried to get her to stay on, but she'd already terminated the lease. Her promise to meet him from time to time offset the cruelty of their goodbyes. For five years, she wrote him letters, refusing email as a precaution. Once a year, they meet when she can get away. Which, of course, coincides with the husband's work trips. The bitterness of Gabriel's lower-tier existence is made worse by the knowledge that Aude's husband is a high-ranking official in the Canadian military. He must have contacts in Luscano's army—Why else had he been posted in Luscano? Probably to help rehabilitate the local military's image after the atrocities it committed in the nineties, when bodies were dumped anywhere, like rubbish. Even by the cemetery gates, leaving him and Castillo to bury the unknown.

GABRIEL TAKES THE STAIRS down to the living room. There, in a corner, at a desk adjacent to the reception area, Aude is bent over a computer the Grecos set up for their guests. Señor Greco is on the phone, taking a reservation, still dressed in his tango attire.

Aude is writing an email. When she senses his presence, she quickly closes Outlook.

"Gabriel, you're up!" She stands to face him. She's blushing, her amber eyes not on him but on Señor Greco.

Gabriel is sure that she was writing her husband and that she knows Gabriel knows. The character in *El Túnel* would make a scene. He doesn't have the nerve. Instead, he asks her what she'd like to do today.

"Let's visit the MALBA," she says. "I will change and meet you down here."

When Señor Greco puts down the phone, he offers Gabriel a coffee. The man leaves for the kitchen, and Gabriel sits down at the computer. It's still open. He clicks on the icon for Outlook, which prompts him for a password. He considers checking his work emails. Better not to know. If there are any burials, Castillo will handle them. Gabriel searches for the Museo del Arte Latinoamericano de Buenos Aires and finds directions to get there by subway.

Señor Greco approaches and hands him the coffee. "We missed you at the tango lesson this morning."

"I wasn't feeling well."

Greco looks over his shoulder at the screen. "The MALBA's a great choice. They have a beautiful café overlooking a park. Good place for lunch. Very Palermo. Just be careful, especially with her. These express kidnappings. They work in twos. First, they separate the couple and take you to banking machines, force you to withdraw. After your cash is depleted, they dump you somewhere if you're lucky, shoot you in the head if you're not. Aude is a target, given her looks. *Obviamente extranjera.*"

Greco adds, "You'll be coming tomorrow, right? It's the last lesson. And, well, the class doesn't work when we're missing a guest. We need the even numbers."

"I'll be there," Gabriel says.

"THIS IS A POET's painting," he says, admiring the lush greens of the portrait.

Aude smiles as he knew she would. "Frida Kahlo would like that."

They regard the artist's don't-mess-with-me gaze, her little monkey, and the parrot at her breast. "She loved her monkey more than she loved Diego," Aude says.

Nearby, there's another portrait by Diego Rivera, not of Frida but of some man, a Mexican, Gabriel presumes.

"He wasn't loyal to her," Gabriel says. "But she was the better artist."

"Frida was not loyal either. She had an affair with Trotsky. I read her diaries, Gabriel."

"I thought you only read poetry," he says. Then he regrets the critical tone. But it's the only absolute about Aude he could cling to. A flame, he thinks, denies absolutes. Always hot, true, but never static.

Later, in the outdoor café next to the museum, Gabriel lights a cigarette and drinks another coffee, his headache lifting. He feels he's been congenial and easy, hoping it's enough to make up for last night.

150

"I was sending an email to my husband," she now says. "I have to let him know I am alive from time to time. Yes, Gabriel? It is only fair."

Fair? *Nothing's fair in love and war.* He doesn't repeat the thought out loud, startled by her mind-reading. Later, he'll thank himself for having kept his mouth shut. When he looks up the statement, it turns out to be a song by a Canadian band called Three Days Grace. And the inverse of what he should have said to Aude, *All's fair in love and war.* A sentiment originating in a sixteenth-century novel, apparently, and a solid reminder to avoid quoting statements of unknown origins.

"He happens to be in Kabul right now. Enough worries there without stressing about whether I am okay."

"Don't you think he knows about us? Don't you suspect he, too, has a lover, maybe more than one?"

"What about you, Gabriel?"

He shakes his head. "I am, and always will be, totally loyal to you, Aude."

"What about this Roma you often mention?"

"Roma?" He laughs. "She'd be appalled if she heard you say that!" He doesn't tell Aude that Roma's gay. Let her think whatever. "What about you, Aude?"

An alarming silence. She's looking out at the park adjacent to the café, where the city's legendary dog walkers are out in full force. A man manoeuvres at least seven dogs on leashes. How does he get them to go in one direction?

Then she says, "Nobody owns me."

The waiter brings lunch. Luckily nothing silly like a serving of soup perched above a frantic goldfish. Gabriel eats the salad, having ordered the same meal as Aude. A last-ditch effort to be conciliatory. Her words sting.

"I understand that, Aude," he says. "I have a mother and a sister. Nobody owns them." He doesn't add that his sister has an annoying husband she should get rid of.

"Tomorrow's our last day," she says. "What would you like to do?"

"El Cuartito," he says without hesitation. "Best pizza in the world. Boxing posters on the walls, tables crowded with porteños from all walks of life. You will love it, Aude. It's not far from the Teatro Colón. We can go inside and take a look. It's a beautiful theatre."

Aude looks at him. Gabriel senses a vast distance between her gaze and his. As far as Ottawa from here, an expanse he'll never cross. She takes his hand. "We'll do this again, as soon as I can. I promise."

Her touch channels the music on the sound system. A man's voice addressing the dance, the brazen metropolis, his very being. Not the old tangos that the Grecos tend to play but more contemporary, mystical, and interesting. He asks the waiter, who tells him it's written by the powerhouse of Borges and Piazzolla.

*So many things have happened to us, the games and the sorrow of loving and not being loved.... Buenos Aires, I don't forget you, tango that you were and will be....*

"We saw Piazzolla play a concert in Central Park," Aude says. "Years ago."

The pronoun *we* slaps him in the face.

THE LAST LESSON begins with a photo shoot in the bar, which smells of stale tobacco smoke this Saturday morning. Señor Greco stoops over a tripod, fiddling with the camera while his wife arranges the couples in suitable poses. Ever the romantic, she makes sure each pair is locked in a tango embrace, their chins angled from the lens. The Brazilians comply readily. The grinning Texan holds his wife in a daring dip, a quivering arm supporting her back. Gabriel grasps Aude. The one thing he loathes more than dancing is having his picture taken.

"*Uno, dos, tres,*" Greco shouts. The flash explodes. "*Otro,*" he says. Then he instructs the students to take their seats. "The photos will be available tonight, after six."

"Last chance to rip us off," Gabriel whispers.

Aude shakes her head as if she's shaking him off.

Señor Greco commences the lesson. He's earned Gabriel's grudging respect over the week. If the Hotel Tango is improvised, the man's knowledge is not. He's a natural teacher, knows his subject intimately, and conveys his passion with conviction.

*Nuevo tango* is today's subgenre. Señor Greco plays an excerpt on the boombox. The human sounds of the bandoneon, the uneven rhythms and circular overlapping themes, are haunting. The Grecos demonstrate, dancing in precise angular moves. An attack and retreat of their private battle. No room for nostalgia here, just suffering and the everlasting tension between ego and soul.

When he dances with Aude, Gabriel works to absorb the tango's vocabulary. For once, he feels his feet connect to his legs, to his torso. Her hand in his, the friction of her satin hips, their proximity and yet their distance. Watching the others over her shoulder, Gabriel notices the ease—maybe even trust—of the couples' embraces. Not just the Grecos but the Texans, the guys from Rio, even the young Parisians. There's an affirmation in how their bodies fit together. Some kind of love they've worked out. Not like him and Aude.

The lesson ends with applause, handshakes, and affection for the Grecos. As Aude chats with the Texan woman, Gabriel picks up a CD and notes the title. *Nuevo Tango: Hora Zero*, recorded by Piazzolla in 1986. He senses a presence behind him.

"You liked this morning's tangos?" Señora Greco asks.

Gabriel admits he did.

"You know what Borges once said? *The tango's a direct expression of what poets try to state in words: the belief that a fight may be a celebration.*"

Later, waiting for Aude in front of the Hotel Tango, Gabriel contemplates the words. His plan, revised umpteen times this morning, is to have it out with Aude at the pizza place. So that, tonight, they can celebrate with the champagne cooling in the Grecos' fridge, ahead of tomorrow's dreaded departure.

The morning is humid and hazy. Not much of a breeze. Pedestrians stream the sidewalks. The narrow street is congested with double-parked delivery trucks. Aude slips out of the hotel, takes his arm, and they head toward the taxi stand. She stops to dig her sunglasses out of her purse.

Gabriel sees the motorcycle idling near the curb. Instinct has him step in front of Aude, but he's too slow. The motorcycle driver has already gunned the engine and is aiming toward them. The guy on the back grabs the purse. They dart up the street.

For once, Gabriel doesn't think before acting. Pent-up hostility explodes in his legs. He takes off after the motorcycle, pumping his arms, his loafers slapping the pavement. Gaining speed, he spots the motorcycle waiting at a red light and hurls himself into traffic, ignoring the honking, shouts, and squealing brakes. The light turns green and the bike takes off toward a truck double-parked in front of a café. Gabriel screams, "Stop them!"

The truck driver, an empty metal tray in his hands, looks up and rams the tray into the back fender of the motorcycle. The bike slides, almost toppling, and the purse falls on the street. The driver accelerates and swerves down an alley.

Gabriel rushes to grab the purse, its black leather gleaming like a prize on the concrete. Then he staggers to the truck, chest heaving, heart pounding. By the time Aude catches up, the truck driver has hurried into the café, returning with a glass of water he tosses into Gabriel's face. First shock, then appreciation. Gabriel holds the purse out to Aude.

"Are you hurt?" she asks. "Can you say something?"

The truck driver retrieves the metal tray from the street. A car approaches, barely squeezing past Aude and Gabriel. "You better move," the driver tells them, "or you'll get run over."

Gabriel limps to the sidewalk. The driver is closing the back of the truck. He's neither burly nor young. A small paunch bulges out between his suspenders. "Give him something," Gabriel says to Aude.

She opens her purse and takes out some pesos, but the truck driver refuses the money. "We're not all bad here, señora. Remember that." He climbs into the truck.

"Gabriel, that was..."

"It's okay. Just give me a minute." A burning sensation creeps down his windpipe into his lungs. The soles of his feet throb, as if his heart has split in two and dropped to his extremities. He sits down at one of the tables outside the café, inhales the smell of empanadas and croissants, finds it bolstering. Aude sits down across from him, clutching her purse. Someone comes out of the café, takes a hose, and starts spraying the tiles.

"I can't do this. Once a year, it's not enough."

"What do you want, Gabriel?"

"I want you to come back to Luscano and…"

"And what?"

"Live with me." A vision of his cramped studio apartment. The sensation of moisture on his ankles. "I mean, we'll find a bigger place."

"Yes, I understand."

Did she just say yes?

"You know I will never leave him. It is not fair to you. I understand that."

She's always been direct. Gabriel abandons the long-winded speech he planned, about honour and commitment, all of which have nothing to do with ownership of the other. Belonging, perhaps, and loyalty. Ironic how they learned the tango only to reach the end.

"Next year we could meet in Panama," she says. "How about that? I always wanted a Panama hat!"

"Panama hats are made in Ecuador, Aude." This time, he thinks again, I'm leaving for good.

# PUEBLO CHICO, INFIERNO GRANDE

IN THE GARDEN, a man in an undershirt tends the fire. He ignites a pile of twigs and paper, then adds larger pieces of wood. The flames build, licking the grills, three rows of them, one above the other. The brick barbecue is six feet wide and his height, with a chimney set against the wall. Years ago, the man, an engineer, designed the structure for this very purpose: a Sunday afternoon *asado*. Many guests are expected on this hot summer's day in late December, the time of fiestas and gatherings. Neighbours are already testing their New Year's *cuetes*. Mini explosions can be heard in the distance, accompanying the crackling soundtrack of the back-garden inferno.

In this city, if you go out alone for a coffee, by the time you get home, everyone knows where you've been (Hotel Salta) and what you ordered (*dos medialunas y un café con leche*). It's not because the place is that small. It's more because you stand out and people pay attention. *Salteños* don't rush around focused on the tasks at hand—a banking errand, work deadline, or grocery run. People look at one another, check out

157

who's sitting in the cafés as they walk by, ready at the drop of a sombrero to stop for a chat and coffee, lunch, or an unplanned excursion. There's a marvellous spontaneity. The downside to the sociability is the propensity to gossip. What was she doing at Hotel Salta all alone? The question rips through the city like wildfire.

Corita, as she's called here, has been delegated to set the table in the garden. She takes her time, making sure the cutlery is straight and equidistant, the wine glasses properly placed. Inside the house, the kitchen is crowded with several women and two men chopping produce for the tomato salad, fruit salad, and a concoction Argentines call Russian salad. Corita avoids the food prep, definitely not her forte. Anxiety levels are on the rise and it's best to lie low. Her beloved has gone to pick up the wine. The guests, family members and friends, are invited for one o'clock, which means most will start arriving around two. In half an hour. She's aware that all these people are coming to meet the new girlfriend from Canada, to inspect and assess her, but she has no idea what they're expecting. She's just hoping, maybe a little too much, that they'll like her.

Several times, she asked how many guests were expected. Each time, she was given a different answer. Fourteen. Sixteen. No, twenty. Corita goes with an approximate average, laying down eighteen forks, knives, and napkins.

"There are not enough chairs," she reports back to the kitchen.

"We'll bring out the missing chairs later," she's told. "The kids will have to eat in shifts."

The man tending the fire is sweating. The flames have died down, but the embers are bright red. Corita brings him a glass of water. They don't speak. Before coming here, she was told that his English is good, that he even reads the *Economist*. But, in the ten days she's been here, he's not spoken to her once. His wife, on the other hand, has been very engaging. Lida speaks to Corita in a polished French she learned from her time in prewar Paris, kept up through the local Alliance Française. The couple both speak German, which would be a solution since Corita's is passable. But she senses that they would prefer not to speak the language.

From inside the house, someone's yelling "Corita!" She doesn't immediately realize they mean her, unused to the appellation they've assigned her. When she does cotton on, she resists. She'd understand if the word they made up were a diminutive. But her real name is only four letters, and they've actually lengthened it, adding some emphasis. The way it's said (*Co-REET-ah*) has an insistent quality, like a brand of chip or cheesie.

Eventually, she reports to the kitchen, where she's asked to cut bread, place the slices in six little baskets, and bring them to the table in the garden. Corita finds a knife and starts sawing at a baguette. A man called Castillo pulls his pickup truck in to the driveway outside the kitchen. He and his wife unload baking sheets of empanadas and place them inside the oven. Squeezing past the food preppers, Castillo checks her out with a gold-toothed grin. "Who's this?"

She puts down the knife and bread in her hands. He stoops to kiss her cheek once. When Corita goes to kiss his other cheek and fumbles, he laughs at her two-cheeked habit from Montréal.

There are too many people in the small kitchen. She escapes with her tray of breadbaskets. It's a trek to the garden, left from the kitchen along the front of the house, by giant rose bushes and a towering fir, then left again along a path toward the gallery in the back. There's a shortcut through the interior of the house, but the family keeps the doors locked. Corita doesn't want to bother them while they're preparing for the asado.

As slowly as humanly possible, she places the baskets at intervals along the table. A man emerges from the side door of the house and greets the engineer by the barbecue. The two speak Slovenian for a few minutes. Then the man ambles over to introduce himself in German. Tall and lean, in his early seventies and with a friendly face, he tells her he's the first cousin of the fire tender. "We grew up together," he says. Then he draws a cigarette butt from his shirt pocket. "I'm Dano. Come, let's sit down here." He gestures to a circle of armchairs in the corner of the garden between the fire and the long table.

Dano lights his cigarette. Exhaling smoke, he says, "So you're the *novia* from Canada." She nods, yes, the girlfriend, and he launches into a series of questions. About her parents, when they left Estonia, how come she speaks German. He says that, when he grew up, Slovenia was part of the Austro-Hungarian Empire, so they were obliged to learn German in school. After a few puffs, he tamps out the cigarette on the stone floor and slides the butt back into his pocket for future use.

Dano tells her about the family, how they left Slovenia and went to Italy, where they waited out the war. Except for his cousin, the fire tender, who was arrested by the Nazis and sent to a concentration camp. Corita knows this, knows the fire tender's father was executed for financing the Slovenian resistance to the Nazi occupation, knows the fire tender spent two years in Mauthausen. She wonders why Dano, a cousin, was spared, but he skips ahead to the immigration story. "After the war, hearing about all the Slovenians settling in this region, I decided to move to Salta along with my brother. I convinced my cousin to emigrate with his family as well. The mountains and climate are as close as we could come to being home. Slovenia is an alpine country, you know. Although it also lies along the Adriatic." Corita can't picture the place, not even on a map.

Dano says he runs a sawmill, has never married, lives alone in a house nearby. "You should come and visit me."

Castillo arrives to relieve the fire tender. He stows his guitar in a laundry room beyond the swimming pool and takes over his duties as *asador*. Boisterous voices precede the arrival of a group of guests. She rises along with Dano to greet them.

The first person she's introduced to is Herr Igel. Stocky with ice-blue eyes and a long duelling scar on his right cheek, he's charmed that Corita speaks German. Frau Igel, however, is Argentine, and the conversation switches to Spanish, much to Corita's relief. She doesn't want to alienate her beloved's family with all this German.

She works to follow the conversation, but her mind wanders to the German man's scar. It resembles an open parenthesis to the left of his mouth and gives Herr Igel a cruel quality. Corita remembers her father telling her about the European duelling tradition. While fencing, young men would deliberately nick each other's faces on the cheek. To ensure the scar would remain visible, a hair would be laid on the open wound. The German's marking bears the trace of such a practice.

When another group enters the garden, she's relieved to spot her beloved's head in the distance. Otokar finds her, takes her hand, and kisses her knuckles. More introductions follow. Corita meets his school friends and their kids, an elderly teacher from the Alliance Française who was also the French consul at some point, a couple from the neighbouring province of Jujuy, an agronomist, and more Slovenians, until she loses track of who's who.

One woman stands out for the way she approaches Corita, like a judge in a talent contest. Rosita is the mother-in-law of her beloved's sister. She's funny, cracks everyone up with jokes that Corita rarely gets, but underneath the extroverted comic, there's grit and acuity.

"I hear you were at Hotel Salta this morning," she says, as if to establish her credentials. The matriarch is so plugged into Salta, she knows everything.

The guests stand around the table, starting in on the wine and empanadas. Kids scamper around. The older ones pass by Corita, tossing her curious sidelong glances and some shy smiles. She starts to worry that the pool is an issue, that a toddler could trip and fall unnoticed into the turquoise waters. All the while, Corita hangs on to her beloved's hand as if it's a life raft.

WHEN YOU'RE FIRST attracted to someone, their family history is the least of your concerns. It's all about the folie à deux, how the two of you interact, make love, crack jokes, and play. She met Otokar in Montréal two years earlier, at a party hosted by Baltic friends of her family. Right after they were introduced, Otokar told her a joke:

*What's the word for someone who speaks many languages?*
*A polyglot.*

*What's the word for someone who speaks two languages?*
*Bilingual.*

*And what's the word for someone who speaks one language?*
*An anglophone.*

His joke, an entry point.

"What are you doing here?" she asked him. She stepped closer, found out he spoke five languages. His origins? Born in Milano, half Czech, half Slovenian, grew up in northern Argentina. She'd never met anyone with origins as convoluted as hers.

"And you?" he asked.

"I was born in Canada, but my parents were born in Estonia," she told him. "We're part Russian, part Estonian, part Baltic German, part French."

She did not say, *I come from a long line of refugees, beginning with the Huguenots, who were kicked out of France.* She did not admit, *I don't know what I am.* Nor did she say, *My mother lived in Brazil and Uruguay and speaks seven languages.* Not right away, that is. She was in her early twenties and still painfully shy. She found out later that he was thirty-two and had lived in Montréal since 1976.

There was dancing the night they met, and she only danced with him. When she left the party, the host reproached her. "It's rude to only dance with one person all night." She didn't care. Next morning, she called her mother, in Ottawa.

"I met a guy," she said.

Her mother laughed. Just two weeks earlier, she'd called her mother saying she was through with men. Her mother had immediately mailed her a card. There was a picture of a shuttered window, a row of plants on the sill. Inside, the printed message read, "I shutter to think…" underneath which her mother had written some words about how nothing is permanent, life changes all the time, the situation you're in today is not the one you'll be in forever. Her mother's trademark Buddhist streak.

Otokar called her a few days after the party. They went out, and again, and again. Her mother cautioned, "It sounds like a straw fire. Be careful. You'll get burned."

Who listens to one's mother when consumed with passion? Months rolled by. Otokar appreciated her independence. He respected her need to write in her journal every night. They went to concerts. Mercedes Sosa appeared in Place des Arts, the audience full of exiled Latinos who sang along to the folk singer's rendition of "Gracias a la Vida," a survival anthem for those who'd escaped torture and incarceration at the hands of the military regimes. At the Montréal World Film Festival, they binged on movies from Latin America. Every time there was a scene—usually stunning—of the Andes, of red-clay rock formations, megacities or villages where people danced at carnivals in the streets, Otokar said, "It reminds me of Salta."

"I want to take you there," he said later, "to meet my family. As soon as it's safe…"

It took almost two years. Those were the years of the Falklands War and the last days of Argentina's military dictatorship. They finally made it to Salta in December of 1984, after the first democratic elections.

During the months preceding the trip, she walked to work listening to Spanish-language cassettes on her Walkman. She didn't realize it was the wrong Spanish, that of Spain the colonizer, not the refurbished, reclaimed, and decidedly more beautiful version spoken in Argentina. "¿Dónde está la farmacia?" the woman's voice intoned into her headphones, *farmacia* pronounced like "farmathia." She practised, not caring about talking out loud while walking down Sainte-Catherine Street.

Now, in Salta, she's reduced to hanging on to her beloved's hand, not getting the jokes, communicating like a five-year-old, asking Otokar for translations. "What did they say?" And, most often, "Why are they laughing?"

All the while, her mother's warning crackles like an unseen bushfire. "Find out if he's been married, if he has a family there. Be careful—you know nothing about him."


KAPOW! KAPOW! KAPOW! The sounds ricochet through the garden. Kids yelp and scream with glee from a wall behind the pool where the laundry hangs to dry. A contingent of adults runs over. Firecrackers are strictly forbidden when unaccompanied by a grown-up. The troublemakers are disbanded, chased to the table, where adults sit elbow to elbow. At one end, Lida presides, elegant and all-seeing. At the other, her husband, the fire tender. He's put on a blue shirt over his undershirt, sits cracking undecipherable (to Corita) jokes to the German man and company. Everyone calls the fire tender Ingeniero, and he is clearly loved. El Ingeniero makes sure his guests' wine glasses are topped up, checks on the fire, where the embers are white now. Castillo's empanadas have long been devoured. One child takes what's left of her empanada in a tiny hand, walks over to the pool. Her father races over to stop her from chucking it into the water. *Basta*, he says, lifting her in one strong arm. Her name is Lucha (or fight).

165

Nicknames are big in Salta. A few doctors are called El Medico. She wouldn't mind if they called her Poeta, but that's not what she's known as here. She's either La Novia or Corita. Some nicknames feel cruel. There's Flaco (skinny), Gorda (fat), Chango (guy), Nariz (nose). There's Pecho (breast), Loco (crazy), Sapo (toad), and Chicha (unknown).

Castillo begins serving the asado's next course—spicy sausages sizzling on the lowest grill. He loads them onto a platter and someone carries them to the table, places a sausage on each of the guests' wooden boards that serve as plates.

Corita, theoretically a vegetarian, has learned to withhold this information. In Argentina, beef is a national treasure, so important it's been rationed domestically to ensure sufficient supply for exports. It's unpatriotic to self-declare one's preference for produce. She's learned to accept whatever's served, take a small bite, and when nobody's looking (she hopes), slide the offensive sausage, innards, or steak onto her beloved's plate.

Meat defines the place, and people wear leather everything—belts, shoes, jackets, wallets, and purses. *Industria Argentina* is down but not out. The economic devastation left by the dictatorship has inflation doubling on a regular basis. One day, a café charges 100 pesos for a coffee. The next day, 200 pesos. Converting the currency, this amounts to an increase from twelve to twenty-four cents, still highly affordable for those like Corita, who are working from dollars. But, for Argentines, it's a disaster.

Just last week, a couple of days before Christmas, she learned what inflation meant for the family's business. One morning, Lida asked her son to drive to a sugar plantation, fifty kilometres into the countryside, and insisted that Corita come along. Leaving the city, they drove for several hours across the plain, into mountain passes, over the river, past vast fields of produce, soya, tobacco, until they reached the entrance of the plantation.

El Ingeniero is an inventor, building custom-made equipment for business and agricultural concerns. He's the creative force while his wife takes care of everything else, such as payroll, finances, and bill collection—the purpose of this road trip.

Navigating a road flanked by ancient poplar trees, Otokar pulled the car into an outbuilding with offices. The plantation appeared to be a thriving concern, more industry than farm, with rows of trucks and tractors parked in the lot, workers coming and going, and the stately mansion in the distance. The three of them waited in a reception area inside the office. Fifteen minutes, then thirty and more, until finally a clerk appeared behind a counter.

Lida went up to him, explained that she was here about the invoice sent many weeks earlier for equipment delivered months ago. The man listened politely and then disappeared into the offices behind the counter. Another hour ticked by. He finally returned. "Sorry señora, the manager isn't available. Please come back in ten days, after the fiestas."

She insisted, but he stood firm. In ten days, the value of the bill Lida was trying to collect would diminish to a fraction of the cost of the work done for the plantation owned by one of the richest families in Argentina.

The mood during the drive back to the city was sombre. The romance of a family business (independent, free of bosses, total control) corroded in Corita's mind. There were bills and employees to pay, suppliers and bank loans to satisfy before Christmas and the New Year. Corita sat in the back seat listening to Lida speak to her son in Czech. Outside, the landscapes rolled by. Towering red cliffs through mountain passes. Villages in the valleys by the river snaking through the plains. Herds of goats crossing the dirt roads. Gauchos on horseback. Against the magnificence, a family's pride tarnished by the failed attempt to collect on a long-owed contract, a humiliation made worse by Corita's presence.

During her stay in Salta, it became clear that the parents, in their early seventies, hoped Otokar would return to Argentina to take over the family business they'd built from scratch. Corita, the novia, complicated matters. Nobody ever said this to her out loud, but a day or so later, Corita was sitting at a table in the living room, writing in her journal. Lida sat down across from her. A silence, and then this: "You know we need him to come back."

Then she rushed out of the room, leaving Corita alone.


IN THE BACK garden, the conversations have heated up as the asado progresses. Castillo brings a platter of steaks to the table. The jokes have taken a back seat to local politics. The governor, one Romero, whose father was governor before him, is trying various tactics to fan the dying embers of the local economy.

"Tourism! That's what's needed," someone says, banging a fist on the table. The glasses jump in unison.

"More subsidies!" another replies.

Corita struggles to follow the debate. Across from her, someone's son, maybe twenty, is digging into his steak. Corita's been told that he just graduated from college. A deep breath, then she asks, "So what are your plans now that you've finished school?"

"Military academy," he says. "I want to be an officer."

The conversation goes nowhere. It's like the other day, when she asked a friend of her beloved, "What about the disappeared? Among all the Argentines abducted and murdered during the junta, how many were from Salta?"

"I don't know what you're talking about," the friend said.

"What about Jorge Cafrune?"

"What about him?" he replied, slamming the conversational door.

Of all the Argentine singers and guitarists she had listened to on her beloved's stereo back in Montréal, Jorge Cafrune was her favourite. The folk songs he sang were of a simple purity, his voice weathered but clear with emotion, not sentimental but profound and sincere, accompanied by his masterful playing on an acoustic guitar. His "Zamba de Mi Esperanza," a cri de coeur during the junta.

Born in the province of Jujuy, Cafrune travelled the countryside, a minstrel of hope during a terrorist regime. Before the junta, in the late sixties, Otokar was home from university and drove the truck north to pick up his father, who'd been visiting a potential client in Jujuy. When Otokar pulled up to a village tavern near the Bolivian border, his father came out and said, "There's a hitchhiker here. He needs a ride to Salta."

They slid over and a man with a big beard and an even bigger guitar case climbed on board. Otokar recognized him right away and told his father, "He's Jorge Cafrune!" The musician entertained them with stories all the way back to Salta.

After the coup d'état in 1976, the military harassed Cafrune. "Zamba de Mi Esperanza" was banned, yet when the audience called for the song at a festival, he went ahead and sang the anthem.

Two nights later, as he was riding his horse along a dirt road, a Rastrojero pickup truck ran him down. Cafrune died within twelve hours.

*Zamba, ya no me dejes. / Yo sin tu canto no vivo más.*
*Zamba, don't leave me / I can't live without your song.*

Castillo tunes his guitar. In the interlude before dessert, he plays folk songs that everyone, except Corita, seems to know. Otokar, on hearing the opening bars, can immediately identify the genre—baguala, copla, chacarera, milonga, vidala, or zamba—just by the rhythm, tempo, and lyric. Some of the guests at the table sing along. Others keep talking. Kids dash around and the neighbourhood dogs, sensing an imminent battle, bark at cats idling in shady corners.


WHAT HAPPENS when two people come from cultures so vastly different that they don't understand each other's reference points? She associates folk music with her university years in Ottawa. Bruce Cockburn, Jesse Winchester, the Good Brothers, Sonny Terry and Brownie McGhee—names that mean nothing to Otokar. "Will the Circle be Unbroken?" "Tennessee Waltz." Bluegrass standards like "I Am a Man of Constant Sorrow." She absorbed the tunes and lyrics, but the genre was waning, a remnant of the sixties and seventies, replaced by disco, then punk. By the time she moved back to Montréal, there wasn't much in the way of live folk music. One option was the Blue Angel, where on Wednesday nights, she'd listen to folk musicians play on the little stage. It was a tawdry place but authentic. She missed the Blue Angel after it closed for good.

Otokar listened largely to Argentine music, probably because he was homesick. After they first met, he invited her over for dinner at his apartment in a downtown high-rise that her friends, who hadn't met him yet but who resented her sudden absence from their little circle, called "bastion of the bourgeoisie." While he cooked, she flipped through his record collection, encountering album covers featuring musicians like Eduardo Falu, Uña Ramos, Jorge Cafrune. Tangos by Carlos Gardel and Astor Piazzolla. Not one familiar name. But she started listening, liked some more than others, couldn't understand the lyrics but felt their heartache or celebration. On a road trip to Vermont in his old grey Honda, Otokar sang a song about a gaucho who loved his horse more than his woman. When it was her turn, she got brave enough to sing. Her bare feet on the dashboard, windows wide open to Lake Champlain's glittering big blues, she serenaded him with a favourite John Prine, emphasizing the line she loved so much, *Ain't it funny how an old broken bottle looks just like a diamond ring?* Maybe she sang that song as a warning. She wasn't in any rush to get married. When it was his turn to sing, he channelled Dávalos, Yupanqui, Sosa, then taught her the Italian lyrics to Santa Lucia. *Sul mare luccica / L'astro d'argento…*

Not to be outdone, she tried to fake her way in Italian when they met after work for dinner at Rotisserie Italienne on Sainte-Catherine. While he carried on long conversations with Giovanni and Rafael, the owners, she pretended to understand, eating her pizza or pasta. The language was so beautiful, she later considered abandoning Spanish for Italian.

Like Estonian, all the vowels made Italian the perfect singing language. Her mother once told her that Estonian was voted the world's most beautiful language for singing.

One night, after pizza, she cracked a tasteless joke. "What's black and white and red all over?"

He shrugged. "No idea."

"A bleeding nun rolling down a hill."

"That's not funny," Otokar said. Another of their interior parallel lines they couldn't connect: religion. He attended mass occasionally, not consistently, but often enough. She didn't go with him until they were in Salta. It felt important to understand the solidly Catholic community.

In the church around the corner from his parents' house, mass featured guitar players and a packed house. Standing room only. Everyone sang the hymns loudly. She understood when a psalm was being read. But, when the priest delivered his sermon, it was largely incomprehensible.

Later she asked, "What was the priest saying?"

"I don't know."

"Why not?"

"I wasn't listening," Otokar admitted.

"What's the point? Why sit through a sermon if you don't listen?"

He never could answer. Nor did he agree with most of the church's dogma. Attending mass, she concluded, was about ritual and community, taking a moment for reflection, a pause before the asados and fiestas, the food, wine, conversation, and music. Later, as he got to know her family, he absorbed her mother's eclectic mix of Buddhism, Sri Chinmoy, Quaker, and Bahai. When she eventually married Otokar, it was in a

Unitarian Church, an institution that does not require conversion.

"They'll marry anyone here," he said after looking at one of their pamphlets.

He knew exactly who he was. She'd assumed, at first, that he felt as much a mongrel as she did. But that wasn't the case.

There was a line in a song she sometimes sang: *My hobo soul will rise.* As if, at some point, she'd be forced to leave Montréal, just like her ancestors had been obliged to leave France, then Germany, Russia, and Estonia. Born in Canada, she didn't feel very Canadian. This unbelonging expressed itself in different ways. When you come from a long line of refugees, you always have a Plan B.

Before she met him, hers was Iceland. If all hell broke loose in Canada, she'd get on a boat and sail to a place where books were cherished, music important, and winter recognizably brutal. But, afterward, with him, she started thinking about Argentina. He was *entre deux chaises*—neither fully of Montréal nor ready to return to a country lurching from one crisis to another. After they met, the pressure from his family to return to Salta began ramping up. She worked on herself. Am I willing to go? It felt like a grand adventure, a possibility for a new life with a new name, Corita.

But, once in Argentina, she started feeling more and more Canadian. Salteños regarded her as an outsider, and she felt so inspected and studied that her misfit persona came into relief. She saw herself through their eyes, and this solidified her connection to Canada. She'd brought some books to read on her first trip. Carol Shields and Alice Munro. Ondaatje's latest. Marie-Claire Blais and Hubert Aquin. Their words her secret passage to her place back home.

In Salta, there would always be the question of her beloved's family, his parents in particular. Moving to Salta would mean they'd live under the same roof as his parents, at least at first. His mother was welcoming, speaking to Corita in French, with a deep sense of charity toward the city's poor. But Lida was also strong willed, one of only two women in her engineering class in Prague. She had rescued her husband from a concentration camp. She had decisive views on things and was accustomed to being in charge.

On her third day in Salta, a good week before the asado, Lida commanded Corita to go buy eggs. Handing her the pesos, she said, "Hurry, go now!"

Corita stumbled up the street, fighting back tears, embarrassed by her hypersensitivity. When she returned with the cardboard tray of eggs, she retreated to her bedroom. Cried into her pillow. Otokar found her, mascara running down her cheeks, and tried to explain. "That's how she treats us," he offered, meaning his sisters and him. "Don't take it personally."

Compounding her anxiety was the enigma of the father, why he didn't speak to her. It took her years to figure out El Ingeniero's resistance, that it had nothing to do with her acceptability and everything to do with the obstacle she posed to his son's return.

CASTILLO CLOSES his concert with a special number just for her. Standing near her place at the table, with his guitar in hand and his golden smile, he delivers a decent medley of fifties rock and roll, "Johnny Be Good" segueing into "Let's Twist Again" and closing with "Blue Suede Shoes." Applause, the wine glasses are refilled, and people start shifting in their seats, arguing, checking wallets for cash, two of the matriarchs staring each other down. Corita doesn't realize war is about to be declared.

Ice cream to Argentines is as important as football, as cherished as mushrooms are to Eastern Europeans or hockey to Canadians. The ice cream shops in Salta put Dairy Queen and Ben & Jerry's to shame. Here, the ice cream is prepared onsite and served in cafés with long glass counters, rosewood ceiling fans, and scents of espresso.

In Salta, there are two camps: Rosemari and Fili. At the table, the sides face each other down, the charge led by two older women not to be underestimated. On one side is Lida, an ice cream lover since her childhood in Prague, for whom Rosemari is the one and only ice cream worth its sugar. She commands her daughter, Paty, to drive to Rosemari and get four litres: vanilla, raspberry, dulce de leche, and chocolate.

Paty's mother-in-law intercedes. Rosita, a force to be reckoned with in Salta, studied in Buenos Aires before settling here with her late husband and, after his untimely death, single-handedly raised three sons while running a chain of cinemas. She commands her son (Paty's husband) to buy four litres from Fili: strawberry, mango, pear, and lemon. The two leave in separate vehicles. A silence drops over the garden. People are wondering if a split might be imminent. Not that divorce is legal in Argentina. But people do split up and it's a mess. Corita has heard about clandestine love affairs, cars parked on the hill in town at night, their windshields steamy, their chassis rocking. At a party, a woman spoke of her husband's lover, who lives across the street from the family home, saying, "As long as he comes home for dinner, as long as he's discreet, as long as he's kind to my mother, I don't care what he does at night."

After the two camps leave for ice cream, Corita helps bring coffee cups from the kitchen. The kids set off a few firecrackers. Kapow, kapow, kapow. A dog howls, as if to a full moon. Some of the guests leave the table for the bathroom. Others smoke cigarettes. An unease prevails. Then a child sidles up to Corita, clambering up the seat to install herself on her lap. The girl's ponytail smells of barbecue, and her hands are sticky. She turns to look up at Corita through dazzling eyelashes. "You peek inglay?"

EL INGENIERO and his wife are, in fact, divorced. Nobody in Salta, except their kids, knows this. It's a carefully guarded secret. Corita watches them interact with each other, two strong personalities who've forged this life, a new life, like so many who emigrated to Argentina.

At the outbreak of the Second World War, Otokar's parents were living in Slovenia with a little daughter. El Ingeniero was supposed to take over his father's businesses. He and his young wife had both studied engineering in Prague, where they had met and fallen in love. Once they graduated, Lida left everything for the more provincial Slovenia. After the Nazis walked into Czechoslovakia, in 1938, she couldn't return.

When the Germans also marched into Slovenia, in 1941, El Ingeniero's father financed the resistance, to no avail. His father was captured and shot; he was sent to Mauthausen while his wife and the daughter fled to Milan. Leveraging her family connections, Lida managed to convince the Mussolini regime to release her husband. Precisely how she did this remains unclear. But, one day, El Ingeniero was ordered to leave Mauthausen and shoved on a train to Italy. At the border, he was shoved off. Wrecked and starving, he was unrecognizable. Lida brought him to their home, near Milan.

Many years later, when El Ingeniero was sitting at the desk in his living room in Salta, he called Corita over and showed her a black-and-white photograph. His hand trembled.

"I took this with my Leica in Milano. I was walking by the Piazzale Loreto and spotted the crowds. Can you imagine?"

He choked up. Corita put her hand on his shoulder to console him, thinking it had to be a photo of his late wife. What she saw was a row of dead bodies hanging from their feet, arms reaching for the ground.

El Ingeniero said, "One of them is Mussolini." The photo was taken on April 28, 1945, two days before Hitler committed suicide.

After the war, the parents returned to Slovenia with their daughter. But, like so many in exile, they returned to an altered reality. In the new Yugoslavia, the family business was nationalized, property seized, the hope of reclaiming their lives dashed. How to get out of this mess?

In the late forties, El Ingeniero got a job in Soviet Russia and left for months. His wife divorced him, returning to Italy with their daughter. It was a ploy to bypass the rules against emigration from Yugoslavia. As soon as he could, the engineer rejoined his family. One year after Otokar was born, they left Italy by ship for Buenos Aires. It was 1951 and Dano was already in Salta, writing letters about how beautiful the landscapes are, how perfect the climate, how full of opportunity.

When they docked in Buenos Aires, El Ingeniero went ahead to Salta to scope things out. Then he summoned his wife.

After a lengthy train ride northwest from Buenos Aires, the train pulled in to Salta. From her window, Lida saw a dusty, forlorn town. Yes, the Andes glittered in the distance, but after Prague, Paris, and Milan, the capital was more than a little plain. At first, Lida refused to disembark. Her husband, standing on the platform, panicked. Just before the train pulled out, he got her, Otokar, and his daughter out and their pile of luggage onto the platform.

Otokar doesn't remember arriving in Argentina or being on the ship from Italy, much less who else was aboard. During World War II, Argentina had aligned itself with the Germans and Italians until, sensing defeat and needing American financial support, the country switched sides. Meanwhile, Nazis escaping the Nuremberg trials with new names and passports issued to them by the Vatican made their way to Argentina, hoping to slip into the woodwork, which they did. Their influence on the military in Argentina is undeniable: how to eliminate dissent or cut off its roots and arrest, detain, and murder Jews, psychologists, activists, communists, journalists, anyone deemed a troublemaker.

Years after her first asado, Corita asked El Ingeniero, "What did your German friend do during the war?" Herr Igel with his duelling scar fit the archetype of an Eichmann perfectly.

His answer: "I never asked."

Nor did El Ingeniero ever meet someone else who'd survived a concentration camp until a flight in the early 2000s, from Toronto to Montréal, the last leg in a journey from Buenos Aires to visit his son. On the airplane, the father was served a snack, possibly a croissant wrapped in cellophane. Already close to a hundred years old, when offered a second croissant, he accepted, commenting to the man beside him, "It's my education from Mauthausen. I never say no to food."

His seat partner perked up. "I was at Mauthausen too."

That was how El Ingeniero became instant friends with Herman Gruenwald, a clothing entrepreneur who lived in Montréal after surviving Auschwitz and Mauthausen.


CORITA WATCHES her beloved's parents all through the asado. They may be divorced on paper, but they interact with a combination of deep love and the exasperation of knowing someone too well. A decade later, in celebration of their fiftieth wedding anniversary and eighty-fifth birthdays, they will secretly remarry in Buenos Aires.

Corita's parents interact in similar ways, possibly more romantically. Every single Friday, without fail, her father brings her mother a bouquet of flowers. They go dancing, write each other love letters. They also annoy each other, those repetitive grievances that love can't transcend. The abrasion of being two entirely different people, who read different books, see the world in their own unique ways.

Waiting for the ice cream to arrive, Corita wonders whether she and her beloved will ever reach that level of deep love. One difference between them and their parents is the absence of cultural references that might connect them during tough emotional intersections. When her beloved quotes epic Argentine poetry, she doesn't get it. When she recites, *Ample make this bed / make this bed with awe*, he doesn't recognize

Emily Dickinson or even know who the poet was. Here, in Argentina, in 1984, she's still the romantic, craving love all the time, sweetness and light, like eating ice cream.

Now, in Salta, battle lines have been drawn. She's stunned to find herself in the throes of an ice cream war, bowls laid out on the table, spoons poising as readied weapons. The litres from Rosemari and Fili are delivered to the kitchen. Lida shanghais the offending products from Fili and throws the litres in the freezer. Only Rosemari will be served to conclude the asado. It's her home, after all.

There's a tension, a watching and waiting at the table. The wine and food have made the guests sleepy. Even the kids are quiet, sitting cross-legged in the grass by the pool, eating their ice cream. Until someone, the agronomist, turns to Corita and says, "*Pueblo chico, infierno grande*," as if the saying—*small town, big hell*—explains the ice cream war away. A burst of laughter and the conversations resume.

During those last days of the year, with fireworks exploding in the distance, various members of the household will raid the Fili ice cream stowed away in the freezer. After making love as quietly as possible in a small bedroom with a single bed, Corita and Otokar will sneak into the kitchen in their sweaty T-shirts, spoons in hand, to savour the mango, the strawberry, the pear, and the lemon, beautifully icy in the heat of the Andean night. On New Year's Eve, the remaining litres are wrapped in newspaper and delivered to a nearby orphanage.

# INSIDE, OUTSIDE

*HERE IN A PRISON cell I outwardly and inwardly revert to the simplest aspects of existence; Rilke, for instance, leaves me cold. Or can it be that one's intellect, too, is impaired by cramped living conditions?*

–Dietrich Bonhoeffer
in a letter to his parents, June 4, 1943

WHEN MY THOUGHTS go to prison, I invariably think of Dietrich Bonhoeffer. In his writings from Tegel Prison's Cell 92, in Berlin, he articulated the dilemma of imprisonment, life lived in confinement, without bitterness. He's been present in my thoughts as far back as childhood, when the idea of prison first entered my consciousness.

It was the summer of 1968. I was seated with my parents and my older brother around the dining room table in our house near Montréal. My brother had just come home from college in Pennsylvania and was describing what it was like in the dorm when a friend's number was selected in the draft lottery.

"Nobody wants to go to Vietnam. And, when their number comes up, the first thing they do is get high or blind drunk. The next day, they call their parents who call their lawyers, friends, contacts in Washington. If that fails, the Quakers will help."

"Anything to avoid the war," my mother said.

"And prison," my father added.

I was perplexed. Justice was simple at the age of ten. You do bad things, you get caught, you wind up in jail. So I asked, "If the law says you have to go, don't you have to follow the rules?"

"The laws can be wrong," my mother explained. "Sometimes a whole government and system are wrong. Sometimes the prisons fill with innocent people and it's the bad ones who remain outside."

This inversion shocked me. Was it possible that we were all the bad ones, and the good people were in prison? My mother invoked the name Dietrich Bonhoeffer, not for the first time. But, on this occasion at the table, I listened. If she had a hero, it was this pastor the Nazis jailed in April 1943. I noticed that, when she invoked his name, my mother's eyes, green as emeralds, deepened. Dietrich Bonhoeffer had been engaged to my mother's best friend. Maria von Wedemeyer was much younger than he was; she had just finished high school. She often told my mother about her prison visits. Maria was feisty, high spirited, and undeterred by the risks of associating with a prisoner of the Nazi regime.

My mother remembered, "She even managed to bring a Christmas tree to the prison. The tree was so large that it didn't fit inside his cell and ended up in the guards' room." She looked from me to my brother. "Never take your freedom for granted."

This was a tall order for a kid; I knew I'd fail as soon as she said this. Even now, it feels impossible to live up to my mother's rule.

*Autumn begins tomorrow.... The changing*
*seasons are harder on one in here than outside.*
    –Dietrich Bonhoeffer
    to Maria von Wedemeyer, September 20, 1943

Ten years after the end of the war in Vietnam, Otokar and I rented a cottage for the summer. We were delirious to find a place in upper New York State for only $100 a month and didn't ask many questions of the recalcitrant owner.

Not that far from Montréal, the thatched cabin sat atop a lawn that sloped to a large lake with a dock. The small property was separated from neighbours by birch trees and unruly brush.

Our first Friday night at the cottage, we installed a new hibachi and croquet set. Otokar fished for dinner off the dock. We drank cheap wine, ate grilled lake trout, and played croquet until dusk. Halfway into the game, Otokar swung his mallet through a cloud of mayflies and whacked my ball into the lake. We splashed around for it in the murky silt then lay on our backs on the lawn listening to the only radio station we could get, country music, and checked out the canopy of stars you'd never see in Montréal. It was only at midnight, when we went to bed inside the cottage, that I realized we hadn't heard or seen a soul. Not on the lake or by the cottages on either side of us. It seemed eerie.

Next morning, we drove into town for some supplies. We passed a convoy of jeeps and military trucks heading toward the base in Plattsburg. They didn't like our little Honda overtaking them on the two-lane road, Otokar driving in his usual gaucho manner. We laughed when they honked and shouted at us.

It was a sunny June day, John Prine singing a waltzy tune on the radio. *It was Christmas in prison / and the food was real good. / We had turkeys and pistols / carved out of wood...* The land was flat here. As we neared the small town, the grazing cows in the pastures dwindled from swaying herds down to one or two staring forlornly through dilapidated fencing.

Dannemora, New York. The name didn't resonate back then. On the outskirts, trailers sagged on scrappy lots strewn with tricycles and tires. There seemed to be more men than women on the streets, and these men were poker-face tough. Even the laundromat and drugstore exuded brutality; battered signs announced their purpose, iron grilles covered the windows.

In the centre of town, a massive wall topped with barbed wire and floodlights rose sixty feet high. Way up in the corner, a guard tower. We could see the men pointing rifles down at us.

Dannemora Prison, officially Clinton Correctional Facility, is the largest maximum-security prison in New York State. It's also known as Little Siberia, and not only because it lies north and the winters are cold. Until 1851, when the iron ore deposits were exhausted, its inmates were forced to work in local mines. In 1900, Dannemora State Hospital was opened for the treatment of prisoners declared insane. Since that time, the single-industry town exists to serve the prison and the asylum.

Driving around the area that weekend in June, we discovered that Dannemora was not the only penal town within hitchhiking distance of our cottage. There were at least four other correctional facilities in Clinton County alone.

It was a long summer. We played croquet and rarely saw our neighbours, who worked in the prisons and were Army reservists in their spare time. On Labour Day, we watched them parachute down into the lake for some kind of military exercise. Then they got drunk and roared around in motorboats. But, all those weekends that summer, when we arrived at the cottage Friday nights, we braced ourselves for a broken window, the flimsy screen door bashed in, and wondered what we'd do if an escaped convict awaited us inside.

Inside, outside. The difference towered in stark relief in Dannemora. Only the guards inhabited both worlds, but they, too, seemed imprisoned by the system.

We're all, to some extent, prisoners of our thoughts, our bad habits, our pasts. After first my father and then my mother died, I realized that, during my childhood, they were still healing from the horrors they'd experienced in Europe during the war. They died, their healing incomplete, but I think they left this world in peace.

A home I once visited in Saigon had a dining room entirely devoted to dead family members, with offerings of oranges, cakes, and candies alongside framed photographs of the dead. Nobody ever ate at the long table with all those chairs left for the ghostly spirits. The space was simply a shrine of remembrance.

In a sense, a shrine is what I have on my shelf now, the collection of twenty-two books devoted to Dietrich Bonhoeffer, including *Love Letters from Cell 92*, his correspondence with

Maria von Wedemeyer. A few letters mention my mother in passing. She and Maria were both deeply into Rilke's poetry and neither could fathom Bonhoeffer's disinterest in the poet. Rilke's complex lyricism, the beauty of his verse might have been too wounding inside the ugliness of prison.

> *This is turning into a wait whose outward purpose*
> *I fail to understand, and whose inward purpose*
> *has to be rediscovered daily.*
>
> > –Dietrich Bonhoeffer to Maria von Wedemeyer,
> > September 20, 1943

DRIVING THROUGH Vermont a few years ago, we stopped at a bookstore in Manchester, where I found a little book about Thich Nhat Hanh, the Vietnamese monk, and his visit to a prison in Maryland.

*Be Free Where You Are* describes the Buddhist's day in October 1999 at the Maryland Correctional Institution, in Hagerstown. After passing through sixteen security checkpoints, the monk arrived in the chapel, where over one hundred inmates were waiting to hear him speak. He began with a silent meditation, then spoke at length, joined the prisoners for lunch, and answered their questions.

In his discourse, Thich Nhat Hanh described the energy of liberation and how to cultivate freedom. He recommended walking meditations, reminding the inmates that the air and sky and earth are the same inside and out. He spoke of understanding and how it makes compassion possible. In a question period, he emphasized poetry as a vehicle for inspiration, encouraging the convicts to write poems to hold close the presence of beauty in their lives.

The book closes with an appendix of letters written by inmates responding to the monk's visit. One man wrote, "His talk penetrated the hearts of hundreds who were in this prison and gave wings to us for flight to a land where wisdom and understanding is the passport and forgiveness is the visa."

Faith and prison are often connected. One hears of ex-convicts attributing their rehabilitation to the discovery of God, either because the prison chaplains are among the rare humans inside willing to suspend judgment and listen or because the convicts are easy targets to proselytizers.

War tested the faith of my parents, with two contrary responses. My mother believed, "I survived therefore there must be a God." My father disagreed, "If there's a God, he wouldn't have let this happen." He was referring to the concentration camps. The war had made an agnostic out of him.

My mother always invoked Dietrich Bonhoeffer to support her belief. Prison didn't break his faith, but he had to adapt his pacifist views and work out whether there was any exception to the commandment, *Thou shall not kill.* He decided that, in Hilter's case, there was, and he actively supported plans to assassinate Hitler. A true theologian can't be dogmatic, must liberate his thinking. How does one do this in extreme circumstances, inside a prison cell?

*Many people have suffered appallingly, and the rest of us, who have been spared, should endure our lesser hardships uncomplainingly and as a matter of course.*

–Dietrich Bonhoeffer
to Maria von Wedemeyer, December 1, 1943

OTOKAR GREW UP in Argentina and went to university in Córdoba, the second largest city, where he witnessed the beginnings of the period of terror. The military burned censored books and shot at protesters on the streets.

Taking a page from Pinochet and his successful purging of dissidents in Chile after the 1973 coup there, the Argentine military began rounding up innocents. Anyone too left-wing for the junta, or too outspoken or artistic or Jewish or listed in someone else's address book... None of their reasons made any sense. It became the horror my mother had described to me when I was eleven, systemic evil. No coincidence that, after the war, Argentina had taken in many Nazis, including Martin Bormann, Josef Mengele, and Adolph Eichmann. According to *A Lexicon of Terror* by Marguerite Feitlowitz, the ex-Nazis "modernized the Argentine secret service."

Camps and prisons filled throughout Argentina. The busiest were located in Buenos Aires, in police stations and military establishments or appropriated civilian facilities such as school buildings. As the Argentine economy tanked and electricity outages plagued Buenos Aires, in order to power the cattle prods used to torture prisoners, the guards had to install generators or rig the devices to vehicles idling on the streets outside. People walked by the detention centres on their way to work. Many believed the military's claims that they were acting in the interest of national security by dealing with terrorists and making the country safe. Others chose not to see.

But the prisoners inside heard the footsteps on the pavement outside. One survivor, quoted in Feitlowitz's book, remembered, "In the afternoon, when the sun was at a certain angle, I could see on the floor the shadows of the people passing by, getting in and out of their cars. Yes, that I think was the worst. To be so close to them, for them to be so close to us, and yet so far away. It was surreal. We were in the world but not part of it, alive in the realm of death."

The detention centres overflowed and the military disposed of the prisoners. Some were dropped alive from air force planes into the sea, others were tortured to death and dumped in fields near the airport. During a six-year period, 30,000 people disappeared. Many others fled into exile.

IN THE MIDDLE AGES, fortresses had underground vaults to dispose of troublemakers. They were called oubliettes. An apt name, drop the prisoner in a hole and forget about them. Not that different from Guantánamo Bay.

This oubliette located on the US naval base occupies forty-five square miles of land forcibly leased from Cuba. The prison is run by the Joint Task Force/Guantánamo with the motto: honor bound to defend freedom. Many of the guards are reservists, from military-police companies, or corrections' employees like those in Dannemora.

Hundreds of prisoners from forty-two countries were brought to Guantánamo starting in 2002. They endured indefinite incarceration, waterboarding, noise stress, and interrogations. There were suicides and suicide attempts, hunger strikes and illness.

And, miraculously, some wrote poetry.

Several years ago, in Seattle, I came across the book, *Poems from Guantánamo: The Detainees Speak,* edited by Marc Falkoff. It's a collection of twenty-two poems written "inside the wire" and cleared by the Pentagon for publication. Hundreds of other poems written by the detainees remain suppressed, considered a special risk to national security.

In the first year of their detention, the prisoners of Guantánamo weren't allowed regular use of pen and paper, so they'd draft short poems on Styrofoam cups using pebbles or dabs of toothpaste. These "cup poems" were passed from cell to cell until they were collected with the day's trash.

Eventually, the military granted the detainees access to writing materials. But many of the poems were destroyed or confiscated by the military.

Shaikh Abdurraheem Muslim Dost, a Pakistani poet and author of many books before his arrest in 2001, is included in this slim volume. One of his poems, entitled "Two Fragments," closes with this couplet:

*I am flying on the wings of thought,*
*And so, even in this cage, I know a greater freedom.*

When Dost was released from Guantánamo, in 2005, the military confiscated nearly all 25,000 lines of poetry he'd written in the prison. According to the editor's introduction, Dost asked a reporter after his release, "Why did they give me a pen and paper if they were planning to do that? Each word was like a child to me—irreplaceable." In October 2006, Dost was again arrested by Pakistani intelligence and, according to the book, has not been heard from since.

DURING THE TWO years Bonhoeffer spent in prison, he wrote books, essays, poems, and hundreds of letters. Even in his cage, he participated in the German resistance, smuggling letters out through sympathetic guards.

Bonhoeffer was moved to the SS prison on Prinz-Albrecht-Strasse, Berlin, in the aftermath of Claus von Stauffenberg's July 20, 1944, assassination attempt on Hitler. Conditions were harsher in this prison. Bonhoeffer was no longer allowed visitors and was subject to renewed interrogations.

When the prison was badly damaged during an air raid, he was moved with nineteen other prisoners, first to Buchenwald then to Flossenburg. On April 9, 1945, Bonhoeffer died on the gallows, in the company of others who had conspired to assassinate Hitler. Three weeks later, Hitler committed suicide.

## THE PAST WAS A SMALL NOTEBOOK,
## MUCH SCRIBBLED UPON

On a winter morning in June, I open the curtains in my hotel room to the city of Salta sprawling toward the Andes. Gangs of gauchos are converging in a plaza down below. Many are wearing large leather shields—*guardamontes*— to protect their legs against thorns, suggesting they've journeyed from afar. They dismount, lead their horses to the fountain for water, and tether them to *tipa* trees. Wrapped in their ponchos, sharing bottles and stories, the gauchos wait.

From my tenth-floor window, the scene is soundless. Doubt creeps in. Is this real or imagined? And why are the gauchos waiting?

I've arrived in the capital of Salta province to attend my father-in-law's one hundredth birthday. Otokar and I came from Canada as we always do, via Buenos Aires, where we spent some days acclimatizing. Actually, there was an ulterior motive to my idleness in Buenos Aires. I'd been waiting and hoping to meet acclaimed filmmaker Lucrecia Martel. Born in Salta in 1966, Martel has written and directed a trilogy of tightly constructed feature-length films shot in her home province.

I've convinced myself that Martel, who now lives in Buenos Aires, is the only director who could take my book and transform it into a film that would outshine the novel. This is a case of hope bordering on the delusional; *Behold Things Beautiful*, about a Latin American poet returning from exile, has yet to capture the imagination of Spanish-language publishers. My hope degenerates as I pass the days waiting to meet Martel.

On our last afternoon in Buenos Aires, I'm in a bookstore in Palermo, not far from the house where Jorge Luis Borges spent his childhood. I browse the labyrinth of book-stacked tables and shelves until I pick up a novel titled *Zama* and leaf through the pages. The book opens with an intriguing dedication: *A las víctimas de la espera.*

The phrase is difficult to translate. The verb *esperar* means *to wait*. It also means *to hope*, which is logical since waiting involves some form of hopefulness. But there's usually also some doubt. Unless, of course, hope is blinded by an irrational faith. Then it becomes delusional.

In a coincidental twist, the bookstore employee tells me, when I'm paying, that Lucrecia Martel is about to make a film version of *Zama*.

On the flight from megacity to provincial capital, I crack open *Zama*. Impressively, it's the novel's seventh edition (Adriana Hidalgo editora, Buenos Aires; 2013). I begin with the author bio and learn that Antonio Di Benedetto, a journalist and screenwriter, wrote nine novels, including *Zama*, first published in 1956. Twenty years later, Di Benedetto was imprisoned by the military dictatorship, tortured, and subjected to mock executions. The hellish wait for release took eighteen months. Later, I learn that the author, arrested within hours of the 1976 military coup, was never told why he had been jailed. Along with many others who managed to survive the dictatorship, he fled to Spain, returning to Argentina after the fall of the junta in 1984. He died two years later, at sixty-three.

The haunting truth is that Di Benedetto's biography corresponds to the fates of many Latin American intellectuals of his time. Persecution by military dictators in Argentina, Chile, Uruguay, and Brazil during the seventies resulted in the disappearances or incarceration of thousands—a form of calculated erasure.


THE PLANE TRIP to Salta takes over two hours. As we fly northwest across the pampas, toward the Andean spine, I'm too absorbed by the book to pay much attention to the stunning landscapes down below. Di Benedetto's novel deals with the fraught causality of waiting, a state that resonates after my days in Buenos Aires.

The antihero, one Don Diego de Zama, is a senior official posted in an unnamed outback of the Spanish realm in the 1790s, waiting and hoping to return to his wife and children in pre-independence Argentina. In the nine-year span of the novel's narrative, Zama lurches from scene to scene in a process of moral degeneration and financial ruin. The longer Zama waits, the more delusional his hope and the more perverse his behaviour.

The novel opens with a riverside scene. Zama observes a dead monkey floating in the rippling water, the corpse rising and falling but not going anywhere, and thinks, *There we were: Ready to go and not going.* To spend time with this unreliable narrator is to submerge oneself in his downward spiral. Zama's wait goes on so long that hope becomes distant, elusive, and eventually, absurd.

When we finally get to Salta and check in to our hotel, I go online and research the book. *Zama*, it turns out, is considered an overlooked masterpiece. Since the fifties, the book maintained a cultish following and was translated into German, French, and other languages. (But not English. It was only later that I found out about an English translation in progress, which was finally released in 2016.)

I also learn that one of my literary heroes, Roberto Bolaño, paid homage to a fictionalized Di Benedetto in his short story "Sensini." Alluding to *Zama* as a novel "written with neurosurgical precision," Bolaño writes that, while critics (mostly Spaniards) dismissed the novel as "Kafka in the colonies," *Zama* endured, recruiting "a small group of devoted readers." Bolaño describes the protagonists of Di Benedetto's fiction as fabled gauchos, "brave and aimless characters adrift in landscapes that seemed to be gradually drawing away from the reader (and sometimes taking the reader with them)."

A FEW DAYS before witnessing the gauchos in the plaza, Otokar and I find a driver to take us south from the provincial capital to Cafayate, a smaller town in fertile wine country. The two-hour journey snakes through mountain passes and crosses largely uninhabited plains where red-hued rock formations stand as immense sculptures, as if waiting to be discovered.

The landscape hasn't changed much in hundreds of years. Except that, this winter, the scrubby vegetation and wide riverbed are parched. A trickle of water is all that's visible of Río Calchaquí, the once tumultuous river celebrated in Salta's music and folklore.

Our driver, Francisco, entertains us with stories as if to distract from the drought devastating his province. Jauntily dressed in a blue cashmere sweater under a leather jacket, he knows the road very well, anticipating sudden turns and narrow river crossings. Like most *Salteños*, he's an affable raconteur. He tells of his past, how he grew up poor in Salta, joined the army at a young age, and made a career for himself.

The dusty mountain landscapes stream past my back seat window to the soundtrack of Francisco's narrative. As it turns out, Francisco served in the honour guard of the presidential palace in Buenos Aires at the time when Isabelita (Perón's third wife) took over as president, in 1974. Her reign, which lasted until the 1976 military coup, is generally considered disastrous, paving the way for the atrocities committed by the junta. When I ask about his role during the dictatorship, Francisco changes the subject to the newly named pope.

"He picked an excellent name for himself," Francisco says, turning to look at me in the back seat. Otokar laughs, and after a few seconds, I get it. The Spanish version of the pope's name is Francisco.

In Cafayate, Otokar stops for a music lesson with his *quena* teacher, and I continue with Francisco to the centre of town. He parks by the plaza and tells me to meet him here in an hour. I'm glad to walk and relieved that he doesn't want to join me. His chatting's become a monologue in urgent need of an intermission.

I circle the plaza, passing benches with backpackers resting their feet and school kids huddling over solar-powered tablets. After visiting a church, I enter an alley that turns out to be an artisanal market. Women sit behind the stands, knitting and chatting. It's the off-season. They're not expecting any business; they're not even hoping or waiting.

I stroll through the alley, then loop back and return to the street. Turning the corner, I catch a blur of Francisco's tan leather jacket before he ducks into a shadowy colonial archway. To shake off my paranoia, I pivot into a side street and enter the first shop. After the brilliant sunshine, it takes some seconds to discern the man with the ponytail and tie-dyed shirt dusting knick-knacks on a counter. There's a basket of *quenas* on the floor. I stoop to check them out. The shopkeeper comes over, picks one of the flutes, and plays a quick tune, his fingers dancing over the holes of the hollow cane, an instrument dating back to the time of the Incas. The Andean melody pierces like a gust of wind over a white-watered river. A tan swath crosses the entrance. Francisco looks inside.

Later, we meet up at the car and Francisco drives me to the quena teacher's house. A nimble rhythm wafts through the open windows, carried by the wind, through the vehicle and up the mountainside, gliding like a condor—all nobility and purposefulness. Francisco is silent, almost brooding. Perhaps he's unhappy that I noticed he was tailing me in the town, motivated, I conclude, by some lingering sense of duty from his days as a presidential bodyguard.

On the drive back, we overtake groups of gauchos on horseback at various intervals. "Where are they going?" I ask Francisco.

Just as the car swerves into a harrowing hairpin curve, he turns to the back seat and looks at me. "To the city of Salta, of course."

I'VE SPENT YEARS trying to discern Salta's complexities. At first, this process was entwined with trying to figure out my husband. Otokar grew up in Salta and left Argentina in 1976. Every few years, we travel back to visit his family, and each time, arriving in Salta, I'm besieged by a conflicting mix of inertia and antsiness.

Part of it is geographic, the recovery from twenty-four hours spent in planes between long sojourns of waiting in airports and adjustment to the city's altitude. Sudden exertions leave me breathless, and my heartbeat keeps me awake at night. Another part is cultural, as I adapt my thinking to Spanish and to Salta's enigmas, such as the distorted notion of time and the casual regard for weapons.

Even though Salta's a city of about one million, everyone seems to know everyone else, or *of* them, which gives the place a self-contained feel. Salteños generally have three or more children, and they have them young, so extended families are large and multigenerational. Not many people born here ever leave, and if they do study or work elsewhere, they often return. Buenos Aires, almost 1,500 kilometres away, feels as detached as a glittering, distant planet.

In Salta, the days exist as long bouts of nothingness between sporadic flurries of activity, an existence held together by the unique texture of an Andean culture with deep Indigenous roots. I learned to speak Spanish here, which only further established me as a naive observer who doesn't totally understand what's going on or get the jokes. No matter how hard I try to adapt, I will always be an outsider, never entirely sure of what's expected of me.

During one long afternoon *asado*, a barbecue of pampa beef, I'm advised by an earnest Salteño that, if I ever discover an intruder in my room, I should "shoot the thief immediately, then shoot at the ceiling so you can tell the police you fired a warning shot." He looks at me expectantly, awaiting thanks for his advice.

In the past, when Salta's quirks, dangers, and weird temporal rhythms perplexed me, I assumed I was just mal-adjusted and/or overly *gringa*. But, in 2002, I saw a film that deepened my understanding of the place.


IN A CINEMA in Montréal, I watched *La Ciénaga* (The Swamp) and saw my various disjointed reflections on Salta explained to me through the lens of an insider's camera. Written and directed by Lucrecia Martel, the film depicts the dramas and inertias lived by two related families. The film's early scene shows the parents stumbling by a pool outside a summer residence near Salta. Kids lie around in a state of heat exhaustion or boredom. Nearby, a band of boys, some armed, track through a leafy forest with a pack of dogs. Thrums of thunder intensify the sense of foreboding.

With close camera shots, Martel captures the family disconnect, neglect, and danger. We're minutes into the film, and the mother, weaving poolside with her wine glass, trips and drops her glass. It shatters on the tiles and she falls onto the shards. She's bleeding, and since the adults are drunk, her daughter, sixteen or so, puts on a shirt over her bathing suit and drives the mother to a clinic. This inversion, where adults depend on their children and children take care of them, is a recurring phenomenon, as is the bleeding woman. Most of the adults, children, and some of the animals in the story are wounded, sometimes fatally. The angles of Martel's shooting style and off-camera dialogue evoke my sensations of being a naive observer of Salta, like a kid trying to make sense of an unfathomable adult world.

The kid's perspective matures into adolescence in Martel's second Salta film. *La Niña Santa* (The Holy Girl) also features a swimming pool, this time indoors, at a decrepit hotel where a medical conference is taking place. Two young women, about seventeen, observe the interactions of the mostly male doctors, some of them blatant sexual predators. Martel plays up the women's hyperawareness and their adolescent fervour, both sexual and religious. The film competed at Cannes in 2004, and when I watched it in Montréal, I looked for and found the signifiers of Salta: Catholicism, incest, and the decaying bourgeoisie.

In the final instalment of Martel's Salta trilogy, *La Mujer sin Cabeza* (The Headless Woman), the point of view ages further, and we see through the eyes of a middle-aged woman. Early in the film, driving alone on a highway, she appears to have struck a dog or a boy. Her head slams the windshield after she hits the brakes. Tightly constructed scenes show the woman, confused and wounded, trying to make sense of her condition but never owning up to the accident. When she learns of the death of a boy on the highway, she admits to her husband that she killed someone. The husband reacts with silence. Her lover, a cousin, handles the cover-up and repeatedly tells her, "Nothing happened." After confessing, to emphasize her willed blindness, she puts on her sunglasses and, choosing not to see, waits out the fallout from the accident.

The 2008 film deals with the morality of indifference and silence. Given Argentina's recent history, it is political with a powerful subtlety. The first time I travelled to Argentina, in 1984, the country had just held its first democratic elections since the dictatorship. Yet, when I asked about the thousands of Argentines who'd been abducted and executed during the preceding seven years, the answer, more often than not, was silence. *De eso no se habla.* Of this, one does not speak.

Martel's trilogy conveys her deeply perceptive awareness of Salta. But, more than a mirror to Salta's middle class, the stories feel universally relevant to me in revealing the degradation of relationships, family life, and society.

In a 2009 interview published in *Bomb Magazine* after a retrospective of Martel's films at Harvard University, the director says, "In Salta, repeating the lives of others is a goal.... In this city, traditions—not in the good sense that traditions can have—are a connection with the past, an affect.... You conserve something that is not alive, something that no longer functions, that is rotten." When I read this interview, a line from *Zama* comes to mind: *The past was a small notebook, much scribbled upon, that I had somehow mislaid.*

History—including the epic battles for independence from Spain—looms large in Salta. But the same pride and spirit that overcame colonial oppression can, over centuries, become degraded and frayed when people cling to traditions that no longer have meaning; they can constrict new generations with untenable expectations. This is what Martel conveys in her films. She introduces elements of the fantastical to raise doubts about reality, giving her films the feel of real experience. The scenes in her movies feel as vivid to me as my interactions with Francisco on the trip to Cafayate.

MARTEL'S ADAPTATION of *Zama*, which she wrote and directed, is her first feature film set outside of Salta. Although Di Benedetto never specifically names his setting, various geographic markers point to Paraguay, especially the river that has special meaning in Zama's state of waiting. Boats arrive with or without his pay, with or without news from his wife, and leave with his messages, his lover, and colleagues, but never with Zama himself.

In an interview in Argentina, Martel recounts how she first read *Zama* during a boat trip on the Paraná River from Buenos Aires to Asunción, in Paraguay. When she finished reading the novel, she found herself in a strange euphoric state that triggered the idea of writing and directing a feature film version. Since then, she's been submerged in the world of *Zama*, comparing the adaptation process to being possessed by a kind of viral infection.

Reading *Zama*, I'm struck by the enormity of Martel's endeavour to transform the book into film. Narrated in first person, the novel is largely internal thought as Zama's situation degrades from that of a high-ranking official drawn into various intrigues with women and his colleagues to that of a participant in, and then prisoner of, a small cavalry bushwhacking into the interior of Paraguay. Zama's shenanigans and convoluted self-analyses are, at times, laugh-out-loud ludicrous.

The story is compressed into three parts according to year, 1790, 1794 and 1799, and it's the final part that evokes cinematic scenes of encampments and the Spaniards' confrontations with Indigenous tribes who tend to show more compassion to their conquerors than is bestowed on them.

In the summer of 2016, the first English translation of *Zama* was published by *The New York Review of Books*. Esther Allen, the translator, spent several years in the anguished world of the novel. She has said that recreating Di Benedetto's sui generis style in English was one of the greatest challenges she faced. When I open the English version of *Zama*, the first thing I do is read the dedication, curious to see how Allen translated the duality of waiting/hoping. It reads, "*To the victims of expectation*," brilliantly capturing the essence of Zama's condition.


AFTER WATCHING the gauchos from my hotel room, I descend into the plaza to see them untying their horses from the tipa trees. They pay no attention to me. The waiting's almost over. Something is about to happen.

The first flank of gauchos rides down the avenue on *paso finos*, horses known for their smooth lateral gaits. Otokar explains that, every year, hundreds of gauchos converge from all over Salta province to file past the monument of their fallen hero, General Martín Miguel de Güemes.

The gauchos in the plaza mount their steeds to join the current of horses on the pavement. A visceral sound from the four-beat rhythms of hooves: we remember, we remember, we remember. I feel the vibrations absorbed in my body; I can still feel them today.

In the fight for independence, Güemes led his cavalry of gauchos against the Spanish royalists in ebbs and flows of victory and defeat. Until, in 1821, under cover of darkness on a cloudy winter night, Spain's army fired a barrage of bullets. Wounded and clinging to his horse, Güemes rode to a nearby ravine and delegated command to his colonel: "Swear by your sword you'll fight for independence until Salta's lands are secured and free." Ten days later, on June 17, the general died.

After the parade of gauchos, I enter Salta's fine arts museum, housed in an elegant early-twentieth-century villa. I am alone except for a security guard who follows me from gallery to gallery. On the second floor, I encounter a portrait of General Güemes. Not the first time I'm seduced in Salta. With his fearless brown-eyed gaze and dark curly hair, the gaucho-commander exudes dashing arrogance and high-octane machismo.

So the rumours whispered by his rivals might be true. His death, they insinuated, was really caused by a bullet fired from a jealous husband's weapon. Güemes might have died for a woman rather than for his loyal gaucho cavalry, another hero corroded by the ambiguity of history.

Not unlike Don Diego de Zama.

At the end of his long wait for deliverance from the hinterlands of the Spanish empire, Zama is arrested and obliged to ride on as a captive of what's left of the ragtag cavalry. The Spaniards are greedy to discover precious gems, called *cocos* by the Indigenous peoples, and deliver them to their imperial patrons. Zama decides to tell his captors the truth:

*"The cocos were an illusion," I said.*
*They did not contradict me with incredulity or*
*mistrust.*
*I had said yes to my executioners, I knew.*
*But I had done for them what no one had ever tried*
*to do for me. To say, to their hopes: No.*

## SOURCES

For the poetry cited in "Braver than Anyone":
Roberto Bolaño, *The Romantic Dogs*, translated by Laura Healy, New Directions; 2008.

For the tangos cited in "Hotel Tango":
Eduardo Romano, *Las Letras del Tango: Antología Crono-lógica 1900-1980*, Editorial Fundación Ross, Argentina; 2000.
The lyrics quoted on the following pages are from these tangos:
132 *Mi Buenos Aires Querido* (My Beloved Buenos Aires) by Alfredo Le Pera and Carlos Gardel, 1934
135 *Barrio de Tango* (Tango Neighbourhood) by Homero Manzi and Aníbal Troilo, 1942
140 *Pensalo Bien* (Think Hard) by Juan José Visciglio, Nola López and Julio Alberto, 1938
143 *Soledad* (Solitude) by Alfredo Le Pera and Carlos Gardel, 1934
146 *Bronca* (Anger) by Mario Battistella and Edmundo Rivero, 1962
152 *Alguien Le Dice Al Tango* (Someone Says to the Tango) by Jorge Luis Borges and Astor Piazzolla, 1965

For the works cited in "Inside, Outside":
Ruth-Alice von Bismarck and Ulrich Kabitz, eds, translated by John Brownjohn, *Love Letters From Cell 92*:

*The Correspondence Between Dietrich Bonhoeffer and Maria von Wedemeyer 1943-45*, Abingdon Press, Nashville; 1995.

Marc Falkoff, ed., *Poems from Guantánamo: The Detainees Speak*, University of Iowa Press, Iowa City; 2007.

Marguerite Feitlowitz, *A Lexicon of Terror: Argentina and the Legacies of Torture*, Oxford University Press, New York; 1999.

Thich Nhat Hanh, *Be Free Where You Are*, Parallax Press, Berkeley; 2002.

## ACKNOWLEDGEMENTS

Many thanks to the editors and publishers of the literary magazines and anthologies where earlier versions of certain pieces in this book previously appeared: *Montréal Serai* ("Braver than Anyone"), *The Puritan* ("Lily Metterling & Her Macho Idiots"), *Grain* ("Don't Tell Pablo"), *Minority Reports: New English Writing From Québec* published by Véhicule Press ("Under the Jacaranda"), *Descant* ("Inside, Outside"), and *Waiting: An Anthology of Essays* published by the University of Alberta Press ("The Past Was a Small Notebook, Much Scribbled Upon").

I also wish to acknowledge the support of the Conseil des arts et des lettres du Québec, which was instrumental in allowing me to complete this book.

I'm deeply grateful to Véhicule Press, especially Simon Dardick, Nancy Marrelli, and Jennifer Varkonyi. It was an honour to work with editor Dimitri Nasrallah and be on the receiving end of his formidable intellect and literary instincts.

To my beloved Otokar, thank you for your devotion and brilliant mind. Here's to our motto: *amor y cachondeo.*

ESPLANADE
*Books*

THE FICTION IMPRINT AT VÉHICULE PRESS

*A House by the Sea* : A novel by Sikeena Karmali

*A Short Journey by Car* : Stories by Liam Durcan

*Seventeen Tomatoes : Tales from Kashmir* : Stories by Jaspreet Singh

*Garbage Head* : A novel by Christopher Willard

*The Rent Collector* : A novel by B. Glen Rotchin

*Dead Man's Float* : A novel by Nicholas Maes

*Optique* : Stories by Clayton Bailey

*Out of Cleveland* : Stories by Lolette Kuby

*Pardon Our Monsters* : Stories by Andrew Hood

*Chef* : A novel by Jaspreet Singh

*Orfeo* : A novel by Hans-Jürgen Greif
[Translated from the French by Fred A. Reed]

*Anna's Shadow* : A novel by David Manicom

*Sundre* : A novel by Christopher Willard

*Animals* : A novel by Don LePan

*Writing Personals* : A novel by Lolette Kuby

*Niko* : A novel by Dimitri Nasrallah

*Stopping for Strangers* : Stories by Daniel Griffin

*The Love Monster* : A novel by Missy Marston

*A Message for the Emperor* : A novel by Mark Frutkin

*New Tab* : A novel by Guillaume Morissette

*Swing in the House* : Stories by Anita Anand

*Breathing Lessons* : A novel by Andy Sinclair

*Ex-Yu* : Stories by Josip Novakovich

*The Goddess of Fireflies* : A novel by Geneviève Pettersen
[Translated from the French by Neil Smith]

*All That Sang* : A novella by Lydia Perović
*Hungary-Hollywood Express* : A novel by Éric Plamondon
[Translated from the French by Dimitri Nasrallah]
*English is Not a Magic Language* : A novel by Jacques Poulin
[Translated from the French by Sheila Fischman]
*Tumbleweed* : Stories by Josip Novakovich
*A Three-Tiered Pastel Dream* : Stories by Lesley Trites
*Sun of a Distant Land* : A novel by David Bouchet
[Translated from the French by Claire Holden Rothman]
*The Original Face* : A novel by Guillaume Morissette
*The Bleeds* : A novel by Dimitri Nasrallah
*Nirliit* : A novel by Juliana Léveillé-Trudel
[Translated from the French by Anita Anand]
*The Deserters* : A novel by Pamela Mulloy
*Mayonnaise* : A novel by Éric Plamondon
[Translated from the French by Dimitri Nasrallah]
*The Teardown* : A novel by David Homel
*Apple S* : A novel by Éric Plamondon
[Translated from the French by Dimitri Nasrallah]
*Aphelia* : A novel by Mikella Nicol
[Translated from the French by Lesley Trites]
*Dominoes at the Crossroads* : Stories by Kaie Kellough
*Swallowed* : A Novel by Réjean Ducharme
[Translated from the French by Madeleine Stratford]
*Book of Wings* : A novel by Tawhida Tanya Evanson
*The Geography of Pluto* : A novel by Christopher DiRaddo
*The Family Way* : A novel by Christopher DiRaddo
*Fear the Mirror* : Stories by Cora Siré